The Girl in the

Sunflower Dress

Katie Montinaro

The Girl in the Sunflower Dress

This is a work of fiction. Names, characters, places and incidents either are the product of the author's imagination or are used fictitiously. Any resemblance to actual persons, living or dead, events, or locales is entirely coincidental.

First paperback edition April 2021
Cover art – Emily Folkard
Clipart - turnip
ISBN print – 978-0-6450918-0-9
ISBN ebook – 978-0-6450918-1-6
Published by Wildflower Publishing

Website: www.katiemontinaro.com

The Girl in the Sunflower Dress

For Maya, Alex and Samara,

Chase your dreams my little sunflowers.

ONE

I have always liked the period between Christmas and New Year; it's as though time itself stands still. Routine and structure seemingly fly out the window, and chocolate is a suitable option for breakfast, lunch and dinner. The clock does not dictate life during this one week of the year.

It's freeing.

Even while I'm working my last shift at Pete's Pancake Parlour, time does not exist. We're busy tonight which is unusual for Boxing Day but it's what keeps time moving at an irregular pace. Time has been…different, since we finished school. If it wasn't for the parlour, I'd have no concept of time at all. Is it Tuesday? Is it lunchtime? Who cares!

Instead of any sort of Christmas bonus or party, Pete has kept the parlour open for an extra few days and agreed to pay us public holiday rates, before closing for renovations. Actually, *renovations* is probably a bit too generous a description; he's closing for a couple of weeks to give the place a much-needed coat of paint and some new furniture. He's told us to expect retro style – whatever that means. Nineties perhaps?

"I can't wait 'til you turn eighteen, and we can get jobs at bars. No more pretending to be happy to clean up little Johnny's mess on the floor *again*." Willow huffs at me.

"Instead, we can just clean up after grown adults who can't handle their drink. No thanks."

Willow pokes her tongue out at me as she scurries off to clean up the spill. She's on the booths tonight whilst I have the other half of the floor. The booths are reserved for families with young kids because it restricts their movements around the restaurant. It's Pete's secret rule but the families never seem to mind; little kids love the booths. It's both a blessing and a curse; booths take twice as long to clean because the kids manage to get food in the most random places. Thankfully my part of the restaurant is filled with families with older children or young couples on dates. There's the occasional old couple but as the night wears on, they tend to be the first ones to leave.

"Just keep thinking of the money," Willow mutters as she makes her way to me behind the counter, carrying wet tea towels.

I'm keeping myself busy wrapping cutlery in napkins as my half of the restaurant is under control.

"We'll probably be begging for shifts soon."

"Speak for yourself! I plan on spending most of the summer lazing by your pool and partying at night."

I roll my eyes. "Didn't get enough of that out of your system at schoolies?"

"It wasn't as fun as I thought it would be, especially without my bestie."

Finishing school – fun. Being only seventeen at the end of school – not fun. Being underage means I missed all the schoolie celebrations on the Gold Coast. Nobody wants to go to schoolies for the underage stuff. Mum and Dad let me throw an end of exam party, but they supervised it, and I didn't feel like partying much. My boyfriend broke up with me just before I completed my exams. Jerk. His schoolie celebrations on the GC were *fun*. As much as I tried to avoid anything Elliott Harrowhill posted online, it seemed to follow me, screaming to be seen.

I saw.

I wish I could unsee.

So far, I have managed to avoid him since he and the others returned. I have a strange feeling in my gut that he is going to show up tonight, as Pete's Pancake Parlour is *the* place to go and is a favourite hangout among our group of friends. If he is going to show up, it'd be tonight, the last night before we close. And if he does show up, I'm not sure if I should throw a milkshake in his face or give him an extra serving of pancakes with whipped cream and chocolate love heart sprinkles.

The door chimes, and Willow and I look up at the new customers. Thankfully, it's not Elliott. I let out a breath.

"Oh my God! Isn't that Noah Kalani?" Willow elbows me.

I nod. He is unmistakable; all long hair, tattoos and a smile that could light up the darkest of nights. His presence commands attention. I've spent many art classes in awe of his…talents.

"Damn it! Regan is seating them in your section. Please let me have them. I've spent the night cleaning up after every little monster. Please, Chels."

"Fine. Fine." Willow hurries away before I even get the words out.

Noah was a couple of years ahead of us at school, and everyone crushed on him so hard. Willow might as well serve them because I wouldn't know what to say to him. Not that we talked or were even friends at high school. He was a senior, and I was a Year 10 student doing senior art as my accelerate subject, so we shared the art room for a year. In that time, I managed to say nothing to him, purely admiring him from afar. We shared a stage together once. We both won top art prizes at school. I think he smiled at me then. That is the extent of my interactions with Noah Kalani.

"My God, that boy is hot! Apparently, it's his birthday. Nineteen. I should give him a birthday kiss." She wiggles her eyebrows at me as she returns.

"Hmm, I don't recall that on the menu…," I tease. "Is that Tommy Tanlon and Zane McIntosh with him?"

"Yes! Zane has turned out to be a mega hottie. Do you remember when we were at the basketball courts, and the ball smacked you in the head, and you had a big lump? He was the one who threw the ball. Remember?"

How could I forget? It's not like it was humiliating or anything. It wasn't just a lump either; it was a bleeding lump. I was sent home because the school was concerned that I had a concussion. Unfortunately, I didn't, and remember the whole embarrassing event.

"He unintentionally hit me with the ball."

Willow waves her hand dismissively. "Yeah, but he came over to check on you. He was totally sweet. Now, he's totally sweet *and* a total hottie. Hot people always have hot friends."

"Okay, well keep it in your pants, you're still on the clock. I don't think Pete wants his pancake parlour turned into *that* kind of parlour."

"As if I'd have a chance anyway. They're like, uni guys, and we've just finished Year 12."

"We're going to be uni girls," I point out.

"Maybe you are, but I'm taking a gap year."

One of my tables starts to look around, a sign that they are ready to order, so I make my way over to them, secretly glad to avoid the uni talk. My ATAR was good, certainly good enough to get into all of the courses I put down. It's just…well I'm not sure *I* want to go to uni. I mean, I want to go, but I'm just not sure what I want to do there. Nothing I put down on my preference sheet was really…me. I just want to spend my days drawing but that is not a suitable option according to my parents.

I wonder what they all ended up doing – Tommy, Zane and Noah? I know Tommy and Zane as well as I know Noah, which is to say not at all, but I know Noah is insanely talented. I wonder if he followed through with his artistic talents and is doing something super amazing and creative. Did any of them know what they wanted to do when they left school, or were they like me, slowly going crazy with the pressure to have it all figured out at seventeen?

Serving Noah is easily the biggest event of the night, although I didn't actually serve him and Willow said no more than, "Hi", "yes" and "enjoy". We still found lots to gossip about behind the counter. Okay, *fantasise* about, behind the counter.

By the end of my shift, my feet feel like they're on fire, and my lower back feels like it is made of cement. Dad is waiting for me in the car park, which is nice, seeing as though he missed Christmas Day at Nanna and Grandpa's house. I give Willow a hug goodbye and climb in.

"Hey, Princess." Dad leans over and kisses me on the cheek.

He places a small box on my lap. The light from the car shows me that it is wrapped in silver wrapping with a red Christmas bow.

"Since I missed yesterday," he says by way of explanation.

I feel a pang of vicarious guilt. Dad has never missed a Christmas until yesterday. and I knew how awful he felt because of it. It wasn't the same without him. It was like there was a gaping big hole in the day.

"Would this happen to be the keys to my very own car?" I try.

Dad lets out a laugh. "You haven't even sat for your learner's permit yet, Chels."

"It'd be an incentive."

"Remember Chels," he says, "hard earned money is twice as sweet when spent." We say the end of the sentence in unison.

"I know! I know!"

"There's no such thing as a free ride, Chels, you have to work hard for the things you want."

I unwrap the box and open it. Inside sits a delicate bracelet with a charm in the shape of a camera hanging off it. "I love it."

"I'm really proud of you, Chels. You've shown you're a hard worker. You excelled in your exams, and you're going on to uni next year. Everything's going to plan."

The plan.

My plan.

His plan.

The *only* plan.

My heart sinks ever so slightly. The plan: ace Year 12, go to uni, get a respectable job, fall in love, get married and live happily ever after with two point five kids. It was the path he took and look how it turned out for him. He has everything I want, including the happy marriage. He has drummed into my brothers and I from a young age that this is the only path to success and happiness. With the first part of the plan ticked off, he'd say I'm on the right track.

I twirl the bracelet in my hands. Photography is our thing, the one artistic pursuit my dad actually has an interest in, and the one thing we do together that is just ours. I like it so much because it's time where I don't have to share him with anyone else. The bracelet is my favourite Christmas gift.

"Maybe some time these holidays we can go shooting further down the peninsula and see what we get."

I nod. "We could go to Point Nepean like we always keep talking about."

It may sound lame, but I actually like spending time with my family – minus my twin brothers. They're annoying. Times two. School and exams consumed me this year, and I know Dad has been busier than ever at work, so I feel like I've hardly seen him this year. I guess being one of the top obstetricians has that kind of effect on your career.

About five years ago, he took a top job in one of the city hospitals which was great for him, but it meant less time for us. It isn't just babies he is expected to deliver; he is running conferences and mentoring other doctors too. I know his job is super important, and we're all really proud of him, but it doesn't make it hurt any less when he misses big occasions like Year 12 graduation or Christmas Day. I try not to complain too much about it; his job means Mum never had to work and could be around for us, and we always have great holidays. I guess that's why our little photography outings mean so much; it's precious time with my dad. Don't tell him, but he's always kind of been my hero.

"I also got these." Dad flashes two tickets in his hands.

I know what I want them to be. I really hope they are what I think they are. I take a closer look at the tickets, and my heart skips several beats.

"The One Hundred Years photography exhibition? That has been sold out for weeks!"

He nods. "Deliver babies for the right people…and it's opening night. Black tie. Canapes."

I lean over and wrap my arms around his neck. "This is the best."

Looks like the summer is shaping up to be a good one after all.

TWO

I'm not very good at sitting still. Everyone talks about this magical time after Year 12 where you get to "rest". *Put in the hard work now and you'll have plenty of time to rest over the summer.* If I had a dollar for every time someone said that to me over the year, I could probably buy the car I plan on becoming licenced to drive. If I'm honest, I like to keep busy, especially now as I try to avoid stalking my ex. I don't mean to, but every time I find myself on social media, I wander over to his pages and immediately regret it. Apparently, he's made it his mission to show everyone just what a #goodtime he's having and how #blessed he is. With nothing much else going on at home, and Willow not returning my texts, I declare myself B-O-R-E-D and catch a train into the city to visit Dad at work, and maybe even sneak in some post-Boxing Day sales shopping.

I grew up around Maternity Wards; when I was little and Dad worked closer to home, he used to take me in with him to do his rounds on the weekends. The new parents never seemed to mind and happily showed off their latest edition. He too was proud to show off his eldest child; he'd tell the new parents that I was his daughter and that I was going to follow in his footsteps one day. I never quite worked up the courage to tell him, let alone his patients, that I had no intention of following in his footsteps. Medical school was never on my radar. Of that I'm certain.

On the Maternity Ward, the nurse tells me I've just missed Dad, so I turn to the elevator in the hope of catching him in the foyer. The doors open, and I hurry in with my head buried in my phone. I press "G" and hear the doors close before noticing the tall, hulking figure slouched in the corner. Keeping my head down, I move to the opposite side of the elevator and feel a set of eyes follow me. The air suddenly feels thick, and I let out a nervous cough. Just my luck to have picked the world's slowest elevator. I avoid direct eye contact yet notice every move he makes. The person cocks his head as though trying to figure me out.

"Do I know you?" a low husky voice asks from the corner.

My heart beating fast, I slowly look up. Our eyes meet, and I let out a sigh of relief. The air around us thins. Yes, we know each other. Kind of.

"Noah?" I immediately know who he is now that I have the confidence to look.

A smile spreads across his face as he stretches out his arms in recognition. "Yep." He clicks his fingers and points at me, "Richardson."

"Roberts. Chelsea Roberts."

I don't mention The Pancake Parlour and neither does he. Seeing Noah twice in two days is more than I've seen him in the last two years since he graduated high school. I'm a big believer in fate and wonder what this means.

The elevator doors open, and he stands back allowing me to exit first. Noah Kalani. He looks just as he did last night, dressed in dark jeans and a Metallica tank baring his tattooed arms. I drag my eyes away to notice him smiling at me. He pushes his dark hair off his face. It falls to his shoulders and looks like it needs a good brush. He's grown a beard, which my dad would call *hipster*, and it ages him into his mid-twenties despite having just turned nineteen. Still, it suits him. I remind myself to blink and return the smile.

And breathe.

"What brings you up here?" I say, surprised, as though he's just turned up to my house.

"Visiting my nan." He points up to indicate she's on a ward.

"Oh," I respond a little embarrassed. I'd forgotten that other things happen here outside of having babies. "I hope she's okay."

"Yeah, she'll be right. You?"

"Visiting my dad. He works here." I point up, needlessly making the point.

"Cool." He smiles.

My eyes dart around, looking everywhere but at Noah's beautiful face. "I thought I'd come up to have lunch with him, but he's not here." Noah nods and his smile broadens. Can he tell I'm nervous? "He's apparently on his way to a meeting."

This is the most we've ever spoken, and I'm messing it up by saying too much. I need to pull myself together. It was much easier last night when all I had to do was admire from afar. Up close and personal, he's intimidating.

Something catches my eye. A man in a charcoal suit across the lobby. Tall, balding and carrying a worn brown leather satchel. Dad.

Thank. God. Something to save me from my embarrassing word vomit.

I point him out and we both look at him as he stops to talk to a lady I don't recognise. A colleague perhaps.

"Looks like your mum found him first."

I let out a nervous giggle. "No, that's not my—" I stop. My mouth hangs open.

What. Was. That?

"Um…shit," Noah appears as shocked as I am. We stand in stunned silence, staring at my dad embracing this mysterious woman whom he has *just kissed.*

In the foyer.

Of the hospital.

In public!

My stomach drops.

Noah grabs my hand and pulls me behind one of the large Christmas trees. It jingles in the commotion.

"You alright?" his furrowed brows try to read my expression.

I imagine it is blank because I can't feel anything let alone what my face is doing.

"You saw that right? You saw them kiss?" He nods. "And it was just like a friendly kiss, right? Like a kiss you give a friend."

"Oh, it was friendly. Like, I'm-screwing-you kinda friendly." He pauses. "Sorry. I didn't…shit." He takes a breath, "what do you want to do?"

I shake my head still trying to process what I saw. "Did she kiss him? Like, did he kiss her back? Maybe it was just…maybe she took him by surprise, and he was just being polite?" My voice rises an octave.

Noah peers around the Christmas tree, and I peer around him, one hand still firmly in his, the other placed on his back. I can see my dad and this *woman* still standing with their arms around each other, talking closely. The woman looks young, maybe in her late twenties, with bright red, glowing lipstick. Her glossy brown hair hangs perfectly down her back without so much as a whisper out of place. I think of Mum, and a sharp pain jolts through my chest. Mum's hair is short, dark and straight, but not glossy. And I don't think I've ever seen her in red lipstick. I lose my balance slightly and fall into Noah's back. He turns around and moves us back behind the Christmas tree.

"I have to follow them."

Noah nods like this is the most logical thing to do. "Do you have a car?"

I shake my head.

"Alright, I've got my car here. I'll take ya."

"You don't have to do that," I protest.

"How else are you gonna follow them?"

I haven't really thought it through. I just have an overwhelming need to follow them. Thinking about it, chances are they aren't going to take public transport, and the second they get in a car and drive off, I'll lose them. I'll be able to follow them to the car park below and that'd be about the extent of my P.I career. I have to take Noah up on his offer if I really want to…do whatever it is that I'm planning on doing.

"Are you sure? Don't you have anything else to do?"

He chuckles. "Just accept the help, Roberts. I'm parked downstairs."

I think it over for a brief moment before accepting. We peer around the Christmas tree again, but my dad and the woman are nowhere to be seen. We walk out into the foyer and briefly look around before looking at each other.

"They must have gone down to the car park."

Racing downstairs, Noah quizzes me on the car Dad drives.

"I don't know. It's black."

Scanning the car park, I realise this description is most unhelpful – every second car is black and looks the same. Noah comes to the same conclusion. "You're gonna need to give me more than that, Roberts."

I search the parked cars for one that looks similar. "Oh! Oh! It has that badge thingy on it."

"A Mercedes?"

I nod. That sounds right. We run through the carpark until we find Noah's car. The word Jeep is sprawled across the two-door white box-looking car with the top already down. I commit it to memory although I was half expecting to be climbing onto the back of a motorbike.

"Do you have like a tracker on your phone or something?"

"What?!"

"A tracker. You know how some parents like to link their phones up to their kids and track them, so they know where they are?"

"We're not like that, Noah."

"Good to know."

We pull out of the carpark and wait in a no standing zone a little further along the road for my dad's car to exit. I look at Noah, he looks at me, and I know that we are both thinking the same thing; what if they've already left? What would we do then? I hadn't thought beyond wanting to follow them. I have no idea what I'm going to do or where it could lead us. What if they're going out for lunch and pack on the PDA in a city café? Or *worse*, what if they go to a hotel together? Eww! I close my eyes and throw my head back on the head rest.

"Oi, Merc. Black. Coming up. This them?" Noah nudges me.

I open my eyes and look in the mirror. I slide down in my seat as I recognise the driver. Dad. *She's* in the passenger seat next to him, in the same spot I was sitting in just last night when he gave me the bracelet I'm wearing. I nod to Noah, and he pulls out after him. He stays back just a bit to give the illusion of space.

Noah and I stay silent as we wind through the unfamiliar city streets. He has to make one of those infamous Melbourne hook turns, and I hide my face in my hands; it has to be one of the most insane road rules ever created! Hook turns and parallel parking are enough to keep me out of the driver's seat, but Noah handles it like a pro. The radio is playing, but I can't make sense of what we're listening to; all of my focus is on the car ahead. Noah lets a couple of cars slip in front of us to keep our cover. We pull up to a set of red lights and out of the corner of my eye, I can see Noah steal a look at me.

"Relax, Roberts." He places his hand on mine making it more difficult to do so.

I realise I have been gripping the seat because as I unfurl my fist, the pain from the tension unfurls with it.

The lights turn green, and we follow Dad's car further into the inner-city suburbs, a place completely foreign to us. We live near the beach on the Mornington Peninsula in a house with a backyard and a pool. This street is wall to wall townhouses with not a patch of blue ocean or green grass in sight. How depressing!

Dad's car pulls into a park outside one of the buildings. Noah does the same only a few spots down, so we are not seen. We watch them walk hand in hand to a tall grey building. Was this his city office? Was she his secretary? Oh, please don't let it be that clichéd.

"Alright Roberts," Noah unclips his seatbelt and turns to me, "now what?"

As this is my first time spying on someone, I'm not entirely sure what to do next. From here on out, I'm relying solely on every spy film I've ever seen to guide my next steps – and I'm not sure that's a good idea. I shrug my shoulders, unclip my seatbelt and exit the car. Noah follows, and we slowly walk down the street towards the building.

"Maybe it's his office?" I offer.

"Why are you whispering?" he returns at a similar volume.

"I don't want to draw attention to us."

"I don't think you have to worry about that."

I look at him confused. "What's that supposed to mean?"

"I mean, you get an early mark from work. You go home with a hot chick. You ain't worried 'bout what's goin' on outside."

I playfully slap his arm. He pretends like I've chopped it off, trying to lighten the mood. It almost works.

"It could be his office." I desperately suggest again.

Noah puts his hands up in defeat as we reach the doorstep. It's gated, and you have to ring one of the nine buzzers to be let in. They could be nine offices. I look closely at the name plates. None say Roberts. I don't know whether I feel relieved or more anxious. Noah is reading over my shoulder and comes to the same realisation. He looks at me for direction, but I don't know what to do. Should I buzz everyone and ask if Doctor Andrew Roberts is there?

"Hey, you know, we could just buzz everyone and ask for your dad." Noah says, as if he read my mind. I give a little smile. He smiles back at me, slightly confused.

There are footsteps behind us, so we move to the side.

"Excuse me," I jump at the sound of Noah's voice, "sorry to bother you, are these offices?" He turns on the charm to the elderly couple who look like they're about to enter the gate.

"No, these are residential apartments. Are you looking for something?"

My heart sinks into my stomach. Residential apartments. Homes.

"Ah, we must have the wrong street. We have a doctor's appointment. My girlfriend here," Noah places his arm around me. It surprises me how light his touch is compared to the size of his arms. "She's pregnant, and we're off to see the, um, lady doctor." I shoot him a look of horror. What. Was. He. Doing?

He looks at me and winks. The couple smile sweetly at us. "Must have gotten the address wrong, hey babe. You don't happen to know if there are any medical suites around here, do you?"

"Sorry, Champ," the elderly man replies, "nothing but residential apartments around here."

"Sorry dear," the lady looks at me with sympathy, "best of luck to you both."

Noah waves them off. "No worries. We'll find it. Cheers."

We pose as a happy, knocked up couple until they're out of sight, and I push out of Noah's arms. I look at him expectantly. He looks pleased with himself as if the situation needs no further explanation.

"What was that?"

"You wanted to know what all this was," he opens his arms as he did in the elevator, as if to say *well here you go.* I lose myself at the sight of his muscles momentarily before I respond. I think he picks up on it because he gives me a knowing smile and flexes.

"Well…thank you. But now what?"

Noah shrugs. "This is your show, Roberts. I'm just your driver."

"And apparently my baby daddy."

He gasps and covers his mouth. "Did you…did you just make a joke?" he mocks me before laughing.

"Alright! Alright! Seriously though, what do I do now?"

He shrugs his shoulders again. I've never been one to like confrontation and have avoided it at all costs. When Elliott dumped me, I didn't yell, scream and demand answers (even though I deserved them!), I just accepted his weak excuses and let him walk out of my life.

I was glad there was no plaque with Roberts engraved on it. It meant I could live in a bubble *a bit* longer. Not his house. Strangely, that was a huge relief. It meant that whatever was going on, wasn't that serious. Maybe it was *just* a colleague who got a bit carried away, and they were actually meeting with other colleagues at her apartment, or in an online meeting. Totally plausible.

"We could sit in the car and wait if you want," Noah offers.

I can't ask him to do that. We don't know how long they are going to be, and besides, this was my family's mess, not his. Another hour of playing P.I., and surely he'll be getting sick of hiding out in his car with some chick from his school, who, up until an hour ago, he'd never even spoken to. Besides, I'm not sure I really want to wait it out. My head is spinning with questions, and my heart is a mix of emotions. I just want to get home and curl up in my bed and forget this ever happened. Not necessarily the Noah parts. We'd had so little to do with each other at school, other than share the art room from time to time, that today has been especially surprising. Noah had a reputation thanks to his short fuse and heated exchanges with teachers and physical run-ins with students. Yet in the art room, where I saw him most, he seemed at peace, lost in his work. I could totally relate. I am the same; whenever I sketch, somehow hours melt away. Art is my refuge. I remember that Noah drew the most amazing portrait of a Hawaiian warrior for his final Year 12 piece to take home the major art prize. The school brought it from him, and it still hangs proudly on display in the admin building. There are rumours that some of the teachers commissioned Noah to create special pieces of art for their own homes once he'd finished school. I guess today I've seen a side to Noah Kalani that his reputation didn't allow at school.

"I think I just want to go home, Noah. I need to figure out what to do next."

He nods. "Okay. I'll take ya home."

"Thank you. Only if you're going that way, otherwise I can train it," I quickly interject.

He smiles. "Accept the help, Roberts. I live down that way too remember."

THREE

The car ride home is quiet except for small talk about music and
Christmas. I'm not really in the mood to talk, and I think Noah
picks up on that. He proclaims to love some song that comes on
the radio and turns the volume up. It stays that way for the
remainder of the trip home. I see him glance over at me every
now and then to check on me, and I glance back to give a
reassuring smile. To be honest, I feel numb; it is as though I am
floating through the rest of the day on autopilot. It only begins
to sink in as we drive down the freeway – *my dad is having an
affair*. He is cheating on his wife of more than twenty years.

My mum.

My devoted, innocent mum.

How can I face her when I get home knowing what I
know? How does he do it every day? My mum and dad met

through a mutual friend at a BBQ one summer. The way he tells it, it was love at first sight. He said he was caught off guard by her killer legs, witty charm, and the brightest smile of anyone he'd ever met. When did he stop feeling that way about her? She certainly hadn't lost any of her beauty and grace with age, and her legs are still killer, but I can't recall any humorous wit in recent times. Maybe that's what having a teenage daughter and preteen twin boys does to you; it sucks the humour out of your life.

Maybe that's what he sees in Miss Glossy Hair. He laughed with her at the hospital. I haven't seen Dad laugh unless he is watching one of those stupid stand-up comedy shows on Netflix where the comedians recycle each other's jokes. Maybe that's the key, humour and fun, because you have fun when you're laughing, right? Maybe they've lost the fun in their marriage? Was that the first sign there was trouble? Maybe I've been too focused on my exams and Elliott to notice my parents drifting apart. Maybe it is our fault, mine and the twins. We ask too much of Mum, and she focuses too much on us instead of Dad. Maybe if we didn't want so much stuff, or to go on big expensive holidays or live in such a big house, then Dad wouldn't have needed to take that job and could have stayed at a hospital close to home; somewhere he never would have met Miss Glossy Hair!

I'm so caught up in my head that I don't realise we've turned into my street until Noah is pulling into our tree-lined driveway. He pulls up outside the garage, puts the car in park but keeps the engine running. I'm not sure if I'm supposed to invite him in. What is the proper social etiquette in this situation anyway?

"You alright, Roberts?"

I nod. "Thank you for today. It was…" I search for the right words.

"Fucked up?"

I sigh. "Sure was." We sit in the silence for a brief moment. "Well, I better go. Thanks again for driving me."

I hop out of Noah's car, and he gives me a half wave. He pauses, looking for the right words to say. I don't think there are any. He settles on, "See ya round," and I wave to him as he drives off.

Today has been beyond surreal. The heaviness of what I saw is really hitting me now; it feels like a weight crushing my chest. And then there's Noah; literally just yesterday he was a pretty face, for sure, but someone I barely knew; now he is someone who shares the biggest secret I have.

As I walk through the door, I find Mum preparing dinner in the kitchen, and I immediately feel my heart hurt and begin to race. I try to avoid her seeing me come in, but it's one of her Mum Superpowers; she sees everything. Especially when I'm trying to hide something. It's like her own spidey-sense.

"Hi honey, how was your day?"

I follow up with one-word answers so as not to give myself away and to cut the conversation short. "Fine."

"Did you see your dad?"

"Nope."

"I thought I heard a car out the front." Sees and hears everything. Superpowers.

"I ran into a friend. We hung out. Dropped me home." Must avoid using the male pronoun to avoid further questions.

"Hmm." She's suspicious. "Why don't you come and keep me company while I cook and tell me—"

"I'm really sorry Mum, I'm not feeling great. I might go and lie down for a bit."

I don't wait for her to respond, instead I take myself upstairs and crash on my bed. I run through the day's events in my head and think about what I know for certain:

1. Mum and Dad loved each other. Once.
2. A woman (a.k.a. Miss Glossy Hair) kissed my dad.
3. Dad and Miss Glossy Hair spent the afternoon in an unknown apartment. Not his.
4. I definitely want to see Noah again.
5. I need a plan

FOUR

The text message alert tone wakes me from my dreams. I am disorientated at first. I find myself lying on top of my doona with my curtains drawn, still dressed in the same jeans and t-shirt I wore to the city, and a light blanket placed over me. Unaware of how much time has passed, I reach for my buzzing phone to see that I have in fact slept through the night and it is now 6.05am. I have numerous missed messages on my phone. My stomach flips wondering what has happened.

W: Urgh! Families are the worst!!!! The dragons are in town and guess who has to share a room with them? Yep, yours truly! SAVE ME!!!

W: Noah Kalani is your friend on FB! WTF?!

W: NOAH KALANI!!!

Noah Kalani and Chelsea Roberts are now friends

W: Chels! Hello??! WTF is going on? Why is Noah Kalani your friend on FB? NOAH F$%&ING KALANI!! He's following you on insta too! You need Snapchat BTW. Spill. The. TEA!

Noah Kalani wants to send you a message

W: CHELSEA! CHHHEEELLLLLSSSSEEEEEEAAA!

W: OMFG! Chels were you with him all night? Is that why you're not texting back? OMG I need deets ASAP!

I giggle to myself at the thought of my best friend being whipped up into such a frenzy over one little follow on social media. Willow had a crush on Noah in high school, wait, scrap that – she had a crush on *everyone* in high school! The perpetual romantic Willow, whose first message came in just after 9pm, would have had a solid nine hours of stalking my socials to see if Noah had liked any of my posts, stalking his pages to see *if* and *when* I started following him, and concocting some elaborate romantic backstory even though she'd probably love the original – minus the whole affair thing. I'm just not ready to tell her the truth yet. I'm not ready to tell anyone the truth yet, so I give her a version of it.

C: Morning, thanks for the wake-up call *grumpy face emoji* Definitely in my own bed ALONE as I have been allllll night. *face with tongue out emoji* Ran into Noah in the city yesterday. My socials are all public so ANYONE can follow them. I also have an Arabian Prince who follows me and propositions marriage every now and then too.

I flip between messages and Messenger to open Noah's message. There's more than a slight flutter of butterflies in my stomach as I open it; it's a damn tornado. I too had a crush on Noah in high school so the fact that he is now following me on social media is more than a little exciting. And yesterday was like a dream (and nightmare), now that I have given myself permission to think about it.

N: Hey Roberts just checkin in. Hope all ok.

I read the message several times with a goofy grin on my face. He sent the message at 10.27pm. He must think I'm a total snob for not replying. I contemplate replying to him immediately. It is ridiculously early however the rules of text messaging do not apply to Messenger. Messenger is a reply-any-time kind of thing whereas text messaging is a reply-during-reasonable-hours-of-awake-time kind of thing, right? With the exception of best friends who clearly have an "anytime" pass for all forms of communication, as do boyfriends. I let myself fantasise about Noah as my boyfriend, and it does little to calm the tornado rising in my stomach. My message tone goes off, and I know without looking that it's Willow, but I'm still looking at Noah's message. What can I say? All is not okay; it might be a new day, but my nightmare is still the same. My dad is still having (or had?) an affair. I don't know whether or not I should tell my mum, and I don't know if I should confront my dad about what I saw at the hospital. Just the thought of talking to Dad about it makes me feel like throwing up.

I type and delete my response to Noah a handful of times. Growing more and more frustrated with myself and with an increasing need to pee, I settle for something brief.

C: Hey! Thanks for checking in. Not sure how I'm feeling tbh. But I see that you're following me on socials #stalker lol!

Before I can regret my message, I throw my phone down on the bed and head for the toilet. It is the quickest trip to the bathroom I have ever taken, as I rush back to see if Noah has replied; unlike Willow, who would take her phone into the bathroom. Utterly repulsive.

He has.

I continue to ignore Willow's message. I'm sure she'll understand.

N: I like the sunflower picture #stalker

I smile. The picture he is referring to is at least a year old and one of my favourites. Dad and I had been out on one of our photography days and came across a sunflower field. I was wearing my favourite navy dress with sunflowers on it, and Dad insisted I have my picture taken, twirling among the sunflowers. I loved that picture just as I loved that day. Whenever Dad and I went out to shoot, he was like a completely different person, a more relaxed version of himself thanks to art – but he'll never admit it. I made that photograph my profile picture until I got a boyfriend, then I replaced it with a picture of Elliott and I together. I make a mental note to change my profile picture back to the sunflower one.

C: *smiley face emoji* You're up early.

N: MI6 called. Wanted to use my special spy skillset

C: *laughing face emoji*

N: *sunglasses face emoji*

C: Well they've got the right man for the job

N: They said I need a partner though. What you up to today?

I stare at the message. I'm pretty sure all my bodily functions have stopped working; brain, heart, the ability to breath – gone. Poof! My brain kicks in and reminds me to breathe, which is funny because the more I stare at the message, the less able I am to do anything. He wants to hang out today! I've got to be cool about this.

C: Nice to see intelligence agencies being a part of the equal rights movement.

N: Well it's a bit hard to convince old people that your partners preggers and needs to see a lady doctor if they are in fact not a lady *sunglasses face emoji*

I laugh out loud and send the laughing face emoji.

C: Well, now that you know where I live, did you want to come over and I can tell you all about my brilliant plan??

I swear, watching those three dots appear and waiting for someone's message to actually come through is a form of torture.

N: Does it involve spy planes and watches that shoot tranquiliser darts?

C: Unfortunately not. I think my brothers have some nerf guns lying around if that helps? BUT I have a pool and it's meant to be hot today...

N: You had me at pool. See you at 11?

C: Perfect xo

Oh no! I throw my phone down, mortified. 'XO'. Kiss, hug? Oh God, please don't reply. Please don't notice. How could he not notice? It's a text message. The boy has proven he can read! *Ohmygodohmygodohmygod!*
Ding!
I stare at the phone. My heart racing. My head shaking.

N: *winking kissing love heart face emoji*

I clutch the phone to my chest, throw myself back on the bed and kick my legs in the air like an idiot. I spend the next goodness knows how long obsessively reading over our brief conversation, smiling. My phone's message tone sounds again, and I remember that I have to message Willow back. She's asking for more details about Noah and wants to catch up today. I briefly fob her off with some story about a family day, throw myself in the shower and panic about what to wear.

So, I lied a tiny bit to Noah about *The Plan*. It's more of an idea made from every Hollywood rom-com I've ever seen. I use my time in the shower to work on *The Plan* and by the time I have shampooed my hair at least twice and stepped out of the shower, I have a fully formed, foolproof plan.

FIVE

My brothers have decided it is too hot for t-shirts and parade around the house in their shorts, leaving a trail of crumbs from the kitchen to the rumpus room as they continue watching the cricket. How anyone can watch one game for five days is beyond me! I call out to them to clean up after themselves which is met with typical sibling abuse. Mum keeps the house pretty tidy, so I don't have too much to put away before Noah arrives, but my sudden attention to detail raises suspicions.

"Someone coming over?" Mum questions me as I run around her at the breakfast bar, tidying up the last of the dishes.

"Just a friend."

She sips her coffee and asks no further questions. She doesn't need to. Her knowing look gets a rise out of me and makes me blush.

"What?" I protest. "Just a friend I went to school with. He's coming over for a swim."

Her grin widens at the word "he". She always liked Elliott but after he dumped me the way he did and broke my heart, she loathed him, as all good mothers would. She's been very subtle, but every now and then, she'll make a comment about me finding a date; the term "moving on" has become a frequent phase around the house.

"It's not like that."

"I didn't say anything." She threw her hands back in protest. He's just a friend." But I wouldn't say no to more.

"Sure, sure honey. Just a friend." Patronising.

The doorbell rings, and I freeze for a second.

"Do-or," one of the twins yells out from the rumpus.

"Thank you, Captain Obvious," Mum sings back.

I'm positive I'm Mum's favourite. The twins are nothing more than smelly, loud, annoying, pre-pubescent tweens. The stuff parenting nightmares are made of, I'm sure.

I decide to wear something casual for our…whatever this is, today. Dresses seem too date-like, and it is far too hot for jeans and a top. Since I talked about the pool, casual pool wear is what I go with. I wear simple cut off denim shorts and a crocheted singlet that sits over the top of my favourite navy and gold bikini. I've thrown my blonde hair into a messy bun that sits high on top of my head and pitch my sunglasses there too for easy access. As I head towards the door, I start to feel slightly uncomfortable about this whole thing. Maybe I should have worn a different top.

"Hi," I smile as I open the door, and my heart does a little dance.

I have to laugh to myself because Noah and I have the same hair style. He too has thrown his hair into a messy form of bun and it makes him look even hotter than when his hair was down yesterday. I think I prefer it this way. Like yesterday, he's wearing a tank top but this time teamed it with board shorts and thongs. His wrists are covered in leather bracelets, and there is a small chain running from his ear lobe to a small cuff at the top of his ear. He is just so effortlessly cool.

And hot. So very, effortlessly hot.

"Roberts." He smiles and shakes his head as he walks in.

A little confused by his greeting, I take him into the kitchen where Mum is making snacks. It is her default setting; as soon as someone enters the house, she begins preparing a plate of food. As she looks up to greet the guy standing over six foot in her kitchen, I see a flicker of surprise in her eyes and a slight colouring of her cheeks. I'm positive Noah doesn't notice.

"Mum, this is Noah. Noah, this is my mum, Helena."

He extends his hand. "Nice to meet you Mrs Roberts."

She takes his hand. "Oh, please, call me Helena." She is definitely blushing, and now I am blushing with her.

Noah looks around and whistles in awe of the pool outside, which can be seen from the kitchen window.

"This is awesome."

"Thank you. So, Noah—" Oh no, here we go with the twenty questions. Noah, who understood her tone perfectly, sits down on the stool, readying himself for the interrogation. I have no way of getting us out of there now. I am left with no choice but to pull the plate of cheese, dips and crackers towards us and take a seat too. "Chelsea tells me you two went to school together?"

"That's right. I graduated two years ago."

Mum nods. "I thought I knew all of Chelsea's friends from school."

This is the only time in my life I'd be happy for one of the twins to barge in and interrupt the line of interrogation. I try calling them to come into the kitchen through the powers of ESP. No luck. Must be just a twin thing.

"We didn't really hang out at school."

I rush to explain. "Noah was an art student. We were often in the art room together. Remember, he won a prize the same year I did for that warrior piece?"

"You remember that?" Turning to me, Noah sounds surprised.

"Oh yes, that was you? That was an amazing piece of art, Noah. Congratulations. You are very talented."

"Thank you, Helena but if I remember correctly, you have a pretty talented artist here yourself."

Mum jumps up out of her seat. "I do! Hang on a minute." She leaves the room.

"I remember your winning piece. That drawing of the meditating woman holding the world in her hands with flowers coming out of her head." I'm stunned. Speechless. He remembers that? "I thought it was pretty fucking amazing."

I was never one of the popular crew in high school, but I wasn't necessarily unpopular either. I was in that group of people who had a lot of friends from different cliques and moved between groups depending on my mood. Because of it, I thought I just blended into the crowd and went about unnoticed. Except in art; in art I stood out. Mrs Maloney used words like "gifted" and "raw talent", words I had always assumed she saved to use with people like Noah, because that's how I saw him.

Mrs Maloney had an open-door policy for senior art students meaning they could come into the art room whenever they had free periods. I always loved when he came into our class to work on a piece, not only because he was good eye candy, but because I could watch him work. He wore a look of intense concentration, as though he was completely lost in what he was doing. I'd steal a look at him every now and then, assured that he was too wrapped up in what he was doing to even notice me. Now, I'm not so sure that he wasn't looking at me too. When I won that prize and stood on the stage with him and four other recipients, it was the first time I ever felt noticed. Perhaps I was noticed more than I realised.

There are noisy footsteps heading towards the kitchen. They are too loud and too many to be Mum returning from wherever she took off too. Looks like my ESP with the twins was on delay and they are coming our way, but now I don't want them to. Noah and I are having a moment, and they are about to spoil it.

"Yes! Kabana and cheese!"

"Oi!" slap, "don't eat it all ya fat pig."

"Shut up." Punch.

"And these lovely pinheads are my brothers. Chris. Cody," I point out to Noah.

"How the hell do you tell them apart?"

I lean into Noah and loudly whisper, "If it's trouble, it's Cody." I pull the plate away from them and back towards us. "Do you mind leaving some for the rest of us?" I snip.

"Who's this?" Cody has a glint of trouble in his eyes.

"My friend, Noah."

Cody sizes him up and looks like he wants to say something but stops. Intimidated perhaps? I know I'll cop whatever he wanted to say later once Noah's gone, but for now Cody remains silent. For his part, Noah is playing the scary stranger perfectly, staring him down with furrowed brows. That look along, with the muscles and tattoos on display, means Cody won't dare take the chance and say something smart to his face. Cody may be many things, but he's not stupid when it comes to the art of war. He's sly and underhanded which means he rarely gets caught for the trouble he makes. It's usually Chris, who's still a bit naïve, that will be the one Cody gets into trouble. The twins do a quick grab and dash, and head back to the rumpus room.

"You're so scary," I mock.

"You better believe it," he winks at me.

Mum returns. I had almost forgotten she left in search of something. She's waving my old sketch pad in her hands.

"I finally found it! You hid it well, Miss Chelsea May."

Not well enough apparently. I try to protest, but Noah is far taller than me and waves the sketch pad above his head. My attempts at jumping up and on Noah to try and get it back are really quite pathetic.

"Please?" his brown eyes look into mine. How can I refuse? I make a motion to say *go ahead* and begin to bite my nails, secretly cursing Mum in my head. She looks proud of herself, and I remember about Dad. I let her have this little victory.

"These are really good, Roberts." Noah is looking at my sketches, like, *really* looking at them. Normally when I show people, they flick through them and make all those impressed noises and tell me they're good, but he is almost *studying* them. He makes it through a handful of pages before I snatch it out of his hands, much to his displeasure.

"Okay, enough of that. Didn't I promise you a swim?" I quickly hide the sketch pad in one of the cupboards below the kitchen sink and move towards the back door.

Noah follows me but turns and points to where I just stashed my drawings. "I'm coming back for that later though."

Outside Noah wastes no time in ripping off his tank, and I try not to be too obvious in my ogling, but dear God, the boy looks good! The tattoos on his arms extend all the way to his pecs covering each one with the same tribal pattern, and…is that a nipple ring? I blush at the thought. He also has some sort of written script tattooed on his rib under his left arm, but I'm too far away to read it.

All too quickly he jumps in the pool. I undress carefully, placing my clothes on one of the lounge chairs, and I can feel his eyes on me, watching, which only makes me more aware of every move I make. I strip down to my bikini and walk into the pool. Although it is a hot day, the water is cold and pricks my skin. We splash around for a bit and make small talk. It surprises me how comfortable I am talking to Noah considering I was way too shy to at school. He just has a way of making everything feel very chill. It doesn't take long until I feel completely comfortable with him.

"So, Roberts, what's this grand plan of yours?" Noah makes his way onto one of the inflatable lounges. I swim over to him and hold onto the side as I discuss *The Plan*.

"Well, I was thinking about everything, and you know, my parents have been together a long time. Like over twenty years," I pause waiting for a response and when I don't get one, I continue, "anyway, that's a long time. And I mean they've been through a lot right, like with Dad's job and us kids. We're all IVF babies. They really struggled to have kids."

"Sounds to me like a couple that should be stronger together from all they've been through." Noah muses.

"Yeah, I know, but sometimes stress gets the better of people, right? And men have affairs all the time."

"Women too," he interjects.

"Right. Point is one kiss doesn't make my dad a bad man. Like, maybe he and Mum just forgot why they love each other. They've focused on me and my brothers for so long instead of focusing on them as a couple." I can see him trying to connect the dots, so I continue. "If I remind Dad about how special Mum is and give them a special night together then he'll remember why he married and fell in love with her in the first place, and flick Miss Glossy Hair to the curb."

"Miss Glossy Hair?" he lifts one eyebrow at me. I've always been envious of people who can do that because I cannot. "And how exactly are you going to give them this one special, magical love night?"

"New Year's Eve. I'll throw a party here. Dad has the night off. I already checked. I'll take Mum shopping, buy her some red lippy and bam!"

I'm slightly offended when he doesn't jump out of the inflatable lounge declaring it to be the best plan ever. Instead, he lies back with his hands behind his head. Muscles on display. I swear, those things are going to ruin me.

"You don't like my plan? You know, they say who you spend New Year's Eve with is who you'll spend the rest of the year with."

"That's a lot of pressure for one night."

"You don't like New Year's Eve?"

"Oh, I like New Year's, but I don't believe in that bullshit. It's one night, like any other night. Hollywood has you thinkin' it's some big, meaningful love fest."

"So, at midnight, you just pash whoever is around?"

"Yeah," Noah laughs, "it's just a kiss. It's not a big deal." Remembering himself, he quickly adds, "if you're single. I don't mean yesterday was no big deal."

"No, it's fine. I get it." I try not to sound too disappointed.

New Year's Eve has always tied with Valentine's Day as the day to have a boyfriend. It's universally known as one of the most romantic nights of the year! Willow and I fantasise about kissing our crushes at midnight on New Year's Eve at some party. It happened for me last year when Elliott kissed me under the stars at midnight at Greg Davidson's beach house. It was the highlight of my year, and the most romantic moment of my life so far.

"Don't get me wrong Roberts, it's a good plan. I get it. Really. Booze. Music. Get the olds to bump and grind. All good."

I laugh. "Bump and grind?"

"Yeah, your mum's a babe. Don't worry, he'll remember pretty quick. Your plan will work."

"A babe!" I laugh even harder.

"Absolutely. If that's how your gonna turn out, whoa! Roberts, you got nothin' to worry 'bout." Noah jumps off the floating lounge and, in the process, dunks me playfully under the water.

We spend the rest of our time mucking around in the pool. Neither one of us brings up *The Plan* again.

Once Noah leaves, I talk to Mum about hosting a New Year's Eve party. She used to throw epic parties all the time. This is the perfect opportunity to be like the old her, the one Dad fell in love with.

"Oh, I don't know, Chelsea."

"I'll do everything. You won't have to do a thing." I promise her.

"Will your new *boyfriend* be there?" Cody teases. I didn't even see him enter the kitchen. I throw a tea towel at him and miss by a mile.

"He's not my boyfriend."

"Oh Noah," he mocks and makes kissing noises, "Oh, Noah, I love you so much. Mwah. Mwah."

"I'm actually going to kill you."

"Stop it, the pair of you." Mum's warning is hollow.

"It's fine, Mum, you have a spare one anyway," I spit out as I chase Cody around the island bench. We continue this little routine where Cody makes fun of me and I chase him shouting death threats until Dad suddenly appears in the kitchen and commands attention. I haven't seen him since the city, and I freeze on the spot. He looks so familiar yet seems like a total stranger. The dad I thought I knew and loved has been replaced by some shady creature wearing his skin as a meatsuit. A shiver slides down my spine.

"Come on you two, enough. Cody, stop pestering your sister. Go tell me the cricket scores."

Cody runs off to the rumpus room and shouts out the scores as Dad kisses Mum on the head. I feel sick.

"Hi Princess," he turns to me, and I legit think I might vomit. I hate secrets. I hate confrontation even more. "How was your day?"

He's smiling at me completely unaware that I know his secret; it's a strange feeling to be able to see right through someone. I would have once described his smile and features as kind and warm, but now all I see is deceit.

"I don't feel so good." I say as I clutch my stomach.

I really don't. I can feel the contents of my stomach rise. I think I might puke. I head to the sink. Mum jumps up, gets a glass of water and hands it to me. She rubs my back and pulls the hair off my face.

"Oh honey, you must have been out in the sun for too long. You do look a bit sunburnt. Did you two put any sunscreen on out there?" she coos.

"Two?" Dad asks, and I vomit.

Just a little, just the water I tried to drink.

"Chelsea had a friend over. I might take you upstairs and lie you down, honey. Get you a cold face washer."

"Anything I can do?"

"No!" I blurt out quicker and louder than necessary. It takes us all by surprise.

Mum shakes her head. "Poor love, she's not well. I've got this. You've been working hard all day." Oh dear God, more vomit rising in my throat, "I'll deal with her."

Mum takes me upstairs and tucks me into bed. She leaves my side for a matter of seconds and returns with a bucket, wet face washer and a hand towel. Another Mum Superpower.

"Too much excitement for one day." She talks to me like I'm five again.

She strokes my head, and I really wish I was five again. Five-year olds have it so easy. I ask for my phone, and she fetches it from wherever I have left it in the house. After assuring her I'll be fine and I can call her if I need her, she agrees to leave me be. I roll over and scroll through my socials to take my mind off my stomach. *The Plan* just has to work.

SIX

Dad has the day off from the hospital, and he's agreed to take the twins to the cricket which leaves Mum and I free to go shopping for the party. The boys left before I woke up which meant I didn't have to face Dad. I don't think my stomach could handle another round. I don't know how long we're supposed to live like this. I invite Willow along on our shopping spree, partly because I feel bad for lying to her yesterday and partly because she's Mum's "other daughter".

Willow plays it cool over the whole Noah thing, not wanting to bring it up in front of Mum, and Mum doesn't bring it up in front of Willow because I begged her not to! I'm hoping the shops are a strong enough distraction so that we can avoid talking about Noah altogether. I just want to keep him to myself a little while longer. It feels like I exist in this strange twilight bubble, or limbo; one world where my family is the same and life is completely normal, and another world where everything has changed and on the brink of collapse. If I let Willow in on that, it'll throw off the whole balance. I'm not ready for my world to come crashing down just yet, not when I have *The Plan.*

By the time we hit the shops, it's busy. There are plenty of things on sale, and I spend some of my Christmas money on clothes and make up. Willow also spends big on make-up, and we're both on the hunt for that perfect party dress although my thoughts are geared towards finding Mum's perfect party dress.

My phone buzzes and I take it out of my bag with anticipation, hoping it is Noah. When I see it isn't him, I screw up my face.

"Who is it?" Willow asks.

"Elliott." I show her the message that simply reads, "Hey".

Mum wants to have a quick look in Target, which is never quick, so we split up and Willow and I head to our favourite shops.

"I didn't think you two were talking," Willow inquires.

We weren't, or we haven't been. Since he dumped me just before my final exam, I've forced myself to cease all communications with him. I've settled for quietly stalking his socials instead. I've been well informed via Facebook that he certainly has been living large since our split and hasn't appeared to be missing me like I am him. His feed is endless posts of parties with girls I don't recognise, lazing on the beach #blessed and generally showing off the wealth his parents afford him. As wild and free as Noah looks and comes across, Elliott is the polar opposite. He's as styled and polished as a Ralph Lauren model. His parents are incredibly wealthy, and it's definitely something Elliott and his siblings aren't afraid to flaunt.

"Should I text him back?" I lean on my best friend for support.

"What do you say to someone who just dumps you out of nowhere, doesn't speak to you for months, and then suddenly texts you?"

I bite my lip. Against my better judgement, I text him back.

C: Hey.

I wait for a reply. When it doesn't come instantly, I curse myself for even engaging with him. It took me weeks to build up the self-control not to text him at any given moment. There were times in the beginning where Willow had to hide my phone because the urge to text him and beg him to take me back was too strong. I've come so far, and yet I feel like I'm about to quickly unravel.

E: What have you been up to?

A reply, but my body doesn't react like it once did. Strange. No butterflies in my stomach. No racing heart. Nothing. Just frustration at his simplistic message.

C: Not much. Shopping with Mum and Will. You?

I knew exactly what he had been doing. Thanks, Facebook.

E: Just hanging out. Been thinking about you. Maybe we can catch up?

Willow is standing over my shoulder reading the messages as I send them. I don't mind, I was going to show her anyway. She lets out a groan.

"Is he serious? Urgh! What are you going to do, Chels?" Willow seems more annoyed than usual.

I shrug my shoulders. "I don't know."

"Are you going to invite him to the party? Are you inviting Noah?"

I haven't thought about it. I haven't actually thought about Elliott at all in the last two days. I was planning on casually mentioning to Noah that he was welcome to come, but I think he'll already have plans. I know I'll be too busy with *The Plan* to entertain anyone anyway. Not that Noah would need entertaining, I'm sure he's more than comfortable wherever he goes.

Willow is coming, and I know she'll be fine. She's been to our house so many times that it is her second home. Besides, she'd be too busy playing the X-Box with the twins to get in the way of *The Plan*. If I invite Elliott, I will have to be sociable and won't be able to keep an eye on my parents to make sure *The Plan* is working.

"I don't think Mum would want him at the house."

"Mum wouldn't want *who* at the house?" Mum sneaks up behind us, and we both jump.

I try giving Willow the wide eyes to tell her not to say anything, but it is too late. Willow caves and tells her about Elliott.

"Sure," Mum shrugs her shoulders indifferently, "the more the merrier."

I look at Willow, stunned. I was sure she'd say no. She wasn't his biggest fan after what he put me through.

"You've both moved on. Just make sure Noah's there too."

Please let there be a black hole that suddenly opens up and swallows me whole. Willow turns to me with heat. I try to avoid her gaze and follow Mum out of the shop. She'll want to know how Mum knows about Noah, and I really don't want to talk about it because talking about it means admitting I lied to her about our family day out yesterday and that means confrontation, and I'd rather poke my eye out with a fork.

"Noah?" Willow goes straight through me, straight to the source. Traitor.

"Yes, he came around yesterday for a swim. Seems like a lovely boy. Very handsome."

Willow widens her eyes at me and places her hands on her hips. Mum forges ahead, and we hang back. All these shops and not one black hole. Someone should talk to management about that.

"What the hell, Chels? *Family day*?" she whisper-yells at me.

My insides turn to jelly. "Sorry. I…I…Dad got called into work at the last minute, and he just showed up—"

"Just showed up?" She doesn't believe me. "How does he even know where you live?"

"He dropped me home after I ran into him in the city. There was a problem with the train line, and he offered me a ride." Seems legit, right? "We just hung out in the pool. Will,

I'm so sorry. I didn't want to tell you because I didn't want you to get mad that I couldn't hang yesterday."

Willow thinks about what I said for a brief moment. "Why didn't you just invite me over? Forget it. Fine. Just don't keep any more secrets."

"Okay," I lie.

"So, what? Are you two like a thing now?" she huffs impatiently.

"No, we're just friends." Not a lie.

"Well, your mum thinks otherwise."

"You know how Mum gets," I offer, but she's still not convinced.

For the remainder of the shopping trip, Willow is upset that I didn't tell her about Noah. Even buying a ridiculously tight body con dress for the party that looks amazing on her doesn't cheer her up. It seems to be really getting to her. If I'm honest, things have been off between Willow and me lately. This is the perfect example of how I can't read her at the moment. We've always been super close and on the same wavelength. We even went through a stage where we finished each other's sentences, but now, our relationship just feels a bit strained. I hope I'm not losing her now school is finished. I offer another apology, and she says she's "fine" about it. She asks again if I have invited Elliott to the party, and I tell her that I'll do it later when I get home. This seems to annoy her even more. Maybe I should tell her about my Dad? If this is how she reacts to Noah, how will she react when she finds out I've been keeping an even bigger secret for longer? I just don't think I can. Not yet. If everything goes to plan at the party then I won't ever have to tell her, and this little blip in my parent's love story can stay hidden and between Noah and me.

Willow doesn't stay for dinner and I take mine up to my room to further avoid Dad. I convinced Mum to buy him a new shirt that matches her dress for the party. Willow and I talked her into buying a lavender frock, one with short sleeves and beading, just short enough to show off those killer legs of hers that Dad likes so much.

I didn't find myself anything to wear so I guess I will recycle an old dress; I'm not sure which one just yet. I flick around my socials and find myself going to Noah's page first. It seems he's not a regular poster and rarely posts pictures of himself, which is a disservice to the community to be honest. There's nothing new on his feed, well not since we've been hanging out. I search a little more and find he is nearing seven hundred Facebook friends, which is a ridiculous amount of people. I also find that he has no photo albums or personal information of any kind on his page. His profile picture is a silhouette (I'm assuming of him) on a surfboard out in the ocean waiting for a wave. There's not a lot on here that really makes it obvious it's his page. If he didn't follow me first, I wouldn't have known this was his page at all. I flip between the different social platforms before I realise that I'm procrastinating and finally message Elliott back.

C: So, my family is having a NYE party. Wanna come?

I don't know why I invite him. I really don't want to see him – which is a new feeling for me. Maybe if I invite him over, it will smooth things over with Willow; she seems more invested in his invitation than me. My phone buzzes. It's not Elliott, and I'm not even mad about it.

N: How'd the mission go Roberts?

I smile. My heart skips several beats, and I immediately text him back.

C: Phase 1 complete. Hot dress for Mum. Tick.

N: And you? *winky face emoji*

C: Nope. I'll just wear something I already have.

N: *sunflower emoji*

This is only going to end in heartbreak, I tell myself. But I can't wipe the huge smile off my face.

C: *smiling face emoji*

I wait. He doesn't reply. I don't want to stop talking to him, but I don't know what to say next. If I double message him, I'll look desperate. It's his turn. Come on, Noah. My phone buzzes. It's Elliott. Disappointment.

E: Love to. See you then *winky love heart kiss emoji*

I roll my eyes and text Willow without too much thought. I tell her Elliott is coming to the party and she replies with a thumbs up emoji, clearly still mad at me. I try not to be too bothered by it because one, I know she will get over it soon enough, and two, I'm desperately waiting for Noah to reply. As the minutes tick by, I can't take it any longer, and I text him again. Hello despo!

C: Did you want to come on NYE? See THE PLAN in action?

He replies back immediately. Was he waiting for me to text him?

N: Sorry. Cant. Have plans.

My heart sinks. I shouldn't have added the bit about *The Plan*. I should have just invited him over, so he knew that *I* wanted him there. I did. I do. I want him there. Another surprising new feeling.

N: Wish I could though *sad face emoji*

I smile. Double message.

C: It's ok. I figured you'd already have plans. *sunglasses emoji*

N: *laughing face emoji* I want a progress report on the night of THE PLAN.

C: Or a debrief the next day?

I write and send it before I realise what I've done. I hold my breath.

N: BOTH! *winking love heart kissing face emoji*

I remind myself to breath. I flick to my Facebook page and immediately update my profile picture. I change it to the picture of me in the field of sunflowers wearing my sunflower dress. Seconds later, Noah Kalani is the first person to like it. I don't think I'm going to be able to sleep tonight.

SEVEN

The next two days in the lead up to the party are a rush. I manage to gather a solid list of Mum and Dad's friends to attend at short notice, and the twins each have a friend coming too. They weren't too happy when I refused their request to invite all of their friends to the party. I have to keep the focus on Mum and Dad rekindling their romance, not Mum running around after the boys and their friends making sure they don't break stuff.

They both seemed less angry about it when I told them Willow was coming, which confirmed my suspicions about their crush on my best friend. Willow is enchanting with her auburn hair, green eyes and freckles; she reminds me of a beautiful pixie. Truth be told, I've always been envious of her looks. When we were fourteen, I tried to dye my locks the same colour as hers with a home kit we bought from the supermarket. It did not end well. I ended up with orange hair, and Mum had to make an emergency appointment with her very expensive hairdresser to correct the damage. I haven't been so bold to dye my hair again, although I'd really love to have pink hair one day. Willow disagrees. She says it's not really "me".

Mum and I spend the day of the party cleaning every inch of the house. We write our to-do list and take great pride in crossing each item off as we complete it. It becomes an addictive game, competing with each other over who can tick the most tasks off the list. I seriously question our mental health.

Noah pops in and helps move things around as Dad is M.I.A. I cringe every time he leaves the house claiming to be going to work. It leaves a metallic taste in my mouth. Each time I wonder if he really is going to the hospital or if he is with *her*. I want to follow him and make sure he is where he says he's going to be, but I can't leave Mum to prepare for the party, not after I promised to take care of it all. I won't lie, the thought of calling the hospital and checking up on him did cross my mind multiple times, but I'm so sure *The Plan* is going to work that I don't want anything to ruin my vibe. I guess it's better not to know sometimes. I wish I didn't know about his affair. Ignorance truly is bliss.

The guests begin arriving by late afternoon. It is an unusually brisk evening which means that people will spend most of the evening inside. Noah spent a few hours yesterday erecting fairy lights by the pool, and it looks magical; it's a shame that no one is brave enough to venture out there to really see it.

Willow arrived this morning and helped with my make-up. Her hair hangs in soft waves around her shoulders, and her dress clings in all the right places. She looks smoking! Thankfully all of the hostility she had towards me the other day has disappeared, and things are back to normal between us. Right up until the other guests arrive, Willow was trying to convince me to wear something other than my sunflower dress.

"I mean, you look great, and it's cute and all."

"But?"

"But it's cute, Chels. Don't you want to look…I don't know. I mean, Elliott is coming," She seems a little frustrated with me.

"So?"

She throws her hands up in defeat. "Sometimes dear bestie you are clueless. Did he like that dress on you?"

I try to think if he ever said anything about this dress. I'm trying hard to also remember why I care about what Elliott thinks. I'm not trying to impress him. Perhaps two weeks ago I would have analysed my outfit and make-up from every angle, but right now, I have bigger things to worry about. Tonight, isn't about me or my dress; tonight is about my parents. Willow finally gives up, and I win the dress battle.

Willow and I head downstairs and join the party. Dad has his arms around Mum, talking to friends of theirs. I snap a sneaky picture and send it to Noah. He sends me back a thumbs up. I'm happy with myself as Willow and I position ourselves in the door frame of the rumpus room where my brothers have the X-Box setup. I can sense that Willow really wants to play and from here, I have the perfect vantage point for spying on my parents (disturbing thought!), so I encourage her to join the boys.

I look over and see Mum and Dad laughing; that's got to be a good sign. I even spy Dad's hand slip further down Mum's back; gross, but surely an even better sign. Success! I tell Willow I'm going to get a drink, but she doesn't respond; she's far too engrossed in the game and beating the boys. Before I move, my phone buzzes with a message from Noah. He's sent a picture of himself holding a beer can up to the screen with the caption *"Cheers"*. I smile and take a quick selfie, making sure to capture some of my dress in the picture and write, *"Back at ya!"* He immediately responds with the fire emoji, and my heart flutters.

"Chelsea."

I startle. I look up from my phone. "Elliott!" I'm surprised to see him standing in front of me. For a brief moment, I forgot that I invited him. He leans in to kiss me on the cheek although his aim is off, and his lips brush the corner of mine. I'm flustered. "It's good to see you."

"You look good, Chels," he smiles.

I panic about what to say next, desperate to drag the conversation away from this dangerous territory of compliments. "Do you want a drink?"

We walk into the kitchen to pour ourselves drinks in plastic cups and sip in awkward silence. Neither one of us knows what to say next. There's too much history between us to begin with simple small talk, and there's too much mess left behind from our break-up to suddenly jump into meaningful conversation. I can't remember the last time I felt this awkward with anyone. Was it always this way?

"Look Chels," I let out a sigh of relief as he breaks the silence, "I just wanted to say sorry about the way things ended between us."

"It's okay," I try to brush it off. It's not okay. It is the furthest thing from okay, but now isn't the time to have this conversation. I'm on a very important mission. And to be honest, this apology is about seven weeks too late. I shift my weight between my legs, feeling frustration build-up in my body. I tense. I shouldn't have invited him.

"I just wish I handled it differently, you know." He reaches out for my hands and I let him take it. "You really are special to me, Chels."

I smile and nod, and take another, bigger swig of my drink. I don't know what to say. Luckily, he does.

"Anyway, I just wanted to say that I'm sorry and hope we can move forward."

I nod again and take another swig of my drink. The alcohol warms my blood and goes straight to my head. My phone buzzes in my pockets (oh, how I love a dress with pockets!). I somehow know that it's Noah. I so desperately want to reach down and read his message, but I can't. Elliott's gaze has me trapped. He lets go of my hand and snakes his arm around my waist, pulling me in for a hug. He places his lips close to my ears and breaths on my neck. I know this move. I know what happens after this move. This move was once my favourite move but not tonight. I begin to gently push him away with an awkward laugh just as my dad walks into the kitchen.

"Elliott, nice to see you." He slaps Elliott on the back as we untangle from each other.

Elliott lets me go and extends his hand to Dad. They exchange pleasantries before my dad excuses himself.

"Excuse me, I have to go and make a call from the study. It's too noisy anywhere else. Great to see you again, Elliott."

"You too," Elliott replies.

My ears prick up. A phone call in the middle of a party? He could be checking in on a patient. Or…the breath that suddenly catches in my throat suggests otherwise. I can feel myself deflating like a discarded party balloon. I follow him to the study anyway. Elliott follows me; he is talking about something, but I'm not really paying attention. I respond with noises to make it sound like I am and pause just outside the study. Dad has left the door slightly ajar, so I pull Elliott next to me and put my fingers to my lips to indicate he needs to be quiet.

"I'm sorry…I know…I can't just leave a party at my own home. Of course, I want to be with you and…don't be like that." It certainly doesn't sound like a patient call. "Don't hang up…don't. Hello? Hello? Shit."

He is coming towards the door, and Elliott and I are standing right there, with no plausible excuse as to why. I grab Elliott's hand and head into the spare room across from the study, shutting the door behind us. So much for *The Plan* working. He was kissing Mum and calling *her*. He was playing them both, he – suddenly I feel lips on mine. Automatically, I follow their pattern.

Elliott is kissing me.

He gently pushes me up against the wall, his hand running up my thigh and up my dress. My leg muscles tighten. I come to my senses and gently push him away.

"What are you doing?" I say trying to catch my breath.

"Come on, Chels."

He comes towards me, putting his hands on my hips, trying to kiss me again. I push him away, harder this time.

"Elliott, stop."

"What the hell, Chelsea? You brought me in here." He's angry.

I feel dizzy. Blood pumps fast around my body. My ears are pounding momentarily making it hard to hear.

"I had to hide from my dad," I try to explain.

"After everything I *just* said…"

"What?" I wasn't listening to anything he just said. Or is he referring to what he said in the kitchen? I can't think straight. I'm too busy thinking about Dad and his phone call. I feel the room tilt. I feel those drinks rising.

"We just spoke about being friends and keeping it casual. I thought you bringing me in here was you saying you wanted it too." His voice is getting louder, angrier. "*You* invited *me* tonight, remember Chels?"

Of course, he hadn't been listening *to* my Dad's phone call. He thought I was listening *out* for him so we could sneak into the spare room undetected.

"You thought I wanted to have *sex* with you?" I try for surprised, but it may have come out as repulsed.

"Why else would you bring me in here?"

Exasperated I reply, "because I was hiding from my dad! I was eavesdropping on *his* phone call. I wasn't listening to *you*!"

"Whatever, Chels. Is it Kalani? Are you two hooking up? Is that it?"

The mention of Noah catches me off guard. Why would he bring up Noah? Then I get it. The only reason he contacted me was out of jealousy over Noah. He must have seen that Noah started following me on my socials and become suspicious. Or territorial? He had been stalking my socials like I have his. It explains why he suddenly felt the urge to apologise to me.

"Everyone's talking about it. He started following you and liking your posts."

"Are you serious right now, Elliott? You dumped *me,* remember? You're the one who has been partying with all these girls and hooking up with God knows who, and you're jealous over one guy liking a couple of my posts on Facebook." I surprise both of us with my little outburst.

Elliott becomes defensive. "I'm not jealous of *him.*" His turn to be repulsed.

I know Elliott, and I know he is jealous. He showed his hand, and he feels threatened by Noah. Good. Maybe he should be. Elliott doesn't want me back and all that talk in the kitchen about me being special was nothing more than him trying to get me to sleep with him. I bet he thought that if he could get his way with me then he'd have one up on Noah. This is nothing more than a game to him. It infuriates me.

"Elliott, I think you should go home." I say calmly.

He lets out a groan. "Chels, you're making a big mistake with Kalani. You're just going to end up getting hurt by him."

The irony. "Thanks. I'll keep that in mind." I open the door and motion for him to leave.

He hits the door frame with his fist on the way out and no doubt did more damage to his fist than the door frame. I follow him out to the front door. He doesn't look back as he leaves, and I don't call out after him. I feel an ache in my chest as I watch him walk away. It reminds me of the last time he walked away from me and while this time it hurts less, it still hurts. First loves are hard to let go of no matter how much of a jerk they are.

When Elliott is gone, I reach into my pocket and finally read Noah's message, although it doesn't give me the same warm and fuzzy feeling it would have half an hour ago when he sent it. It's another picture of him, this time he's sculling a beer.

He has his hair up just like he did the other day, and I find him ridiculously adorable in the photo. I sigh.

C: I need a few of those. Mission fail.

I head back towards the rumpus room to find Willow. She's still playing the X-Box much to the delight of the preteen boys surrounding her. I flop onto the couch next to my best friend, defeated. I rest my head on her shoulder.

N: Faaaaaarrrrrrrkkkkkk. I com get u an we coul get farked up togethre but no state 2 drive

It was obvious from his message that he was in no state to drive, but I appreciated the sentiment all the same. My phone buzzes and it is another picture of Noah downing a different drink with the caption *"get on it stuff em"*. He's clearly had a few too many drinks, yet still manages to avoid looking like a drunken mess in his photos. The guy probably didn't take a bad photo no matter what he was doing. I grab Willow's arm and drag her away, much to the protests of the boys.

"Hey, what's up?" she looks worried.

"Let's go, I need a drink."

"Did Elliott come?" Willow asks, hopeful.

"Yep. Let's go outside, and I'll tell you all about it."

"With drinks?"

"With lots of drinks."

Willow punches her fist into the air and lets out a "Woohoo" as we sneak off for our own private party.

EIGHT

The knock at the door is what wakes me. It is unnecessarily loud and the room ridiculously bright. I squint as the person opens my bedroom door.

"Hey Chels…" I groan as I realise it is my brother. I am too hungover to notice or care which one it is, "your boyfriend's downstairs." Cody.

"What?" I bolt upright, and I immediately feel dizzy.

"Oh, Noah, mwah, mwah," Cody teases.

I throw a pillow in his direction and miss miserably.

"Oi, don't be a dick to your sister." The low voice surprises and excites me at the same time.

Willow gasps and sinks further under the sheets. Noah knuckles Cody's hair and walks past him into my bedroom. He lays himself down on the end of my bed. "See ya little bro." He waves Cody off and to my surprise, Cody obeys and even shuts the door.

The room continues to spin so I put my head in my hands and rub my temples.

"Is Noah Kalani really in your room right now, or am I dreaming?" Willow's muffled voice comes from below the sheets.

"Both, Willow."

"How does he know my name?"

Noah chuckles.

"How are you not hungover?" I groan and lie back down.

"Clearly Princess, I've had more experience at this than you. You know, your room is not at all how I pictured it to be."

He's pictured my room. This sends butterflies to places much lower than my stomach. I sit back up thankful that I went to sleep in my new pyjama top and not my regular t-shirt with holes in it.

"What are you doing here, Noah?"

"Debrief." He states as a matter of fact. "Did you forget?"

Yes. Yes, I had.

"Seriously, how do you know my name?" Willow peaks out from under the sheets.

Noah motions towards my bedside table. "You should check your phone."

Willow and I look to each other, sharing a nervous glance. I remember sending a couple of messages to Noah, but I don't remember what they said. To be honest, I don't remember much of the night after Elliott left. I wish I could forget the part before he left too.

I grab my phone and open the message thread between myself and Noah. I scroll up to the last message I remember sending which was a picture of Willow and I doing shots. He had asked who the red head was, and I told him. That's how he knows her name. One mystery solved.

We had exchanged a series of flirty messages, along with random pictures of the night I cannot remember. I regret them all. There's nothing pretty about them although I probably thought differently at the time. I blame the vodka. I stop at a picture of Noah winking with his lips pursed together making a kissing face. It's stamped at 12.01am. The caption reads, *"Heres ur NYE kissss."* I look at him, and he is stroking his beard with one eyebrow raised, no doubt trying to figure out what part of the message thread I'm up to. If the room wasn't spinning and Willow wasn't here, I'd reach over and kiss him in real life. Or at least I'd like to think I would. I look back at my phone and keep scrolling. I see I responded with a similar picture looking anything but sexy. I look very drunk. I groan with embarrassment as the messages and pictures continue. I pause on a picture of Willow and I in the bed together. We are trying to do our best sexy duck pout faces and bedroom eyes but it's coming off so wrong; so hilariously and embarrassingly wrong. I put my face in my hands and hold the phone out to Noah.

"Oh no," I grumble.

Noah lets out a deep laugh. "That was definitely one of my favourites."

"It's just so embarrassing."

"Do I want to know?" Willow pipes up.

"No," I say. She groans and rolls over pulling more of the sheets over her head leaving me with very little coverage over my bare legs. Noah looks and quickly looks away with a grin on his face.

"Please don't tell me *any* of these ended up online."

Noah shakes his head. "Nope."

I let out a sigh of relief. Thank goodness I had enough sense not to post anything to my socials last night.

"I think I need something to eat." I say grabbing at my stomach.

Noah hits the fitted sheets next to my bare legs. "Then rise and shine, baby girl."

"You're way too fresh for how much I assume you drank last night." A mischievous smile spreads across his face. "You'll need to turn around while I get up."

"Why?" He smirks.

"Because I have no pants on."

His grin widens, and he does that one eyebrow thing again. I playfully hit him on the arm.

"Up and around, Mister!"

Noah gives me a salute and then some privacy. I find a pair of shorts on the ground and quickly throw them on. I let him know he can turn back around as I fix my hair into a top knot.

"You coming, Will?" I ask.

"No. I think I'll stay here and die quietly."

My first steps are slightly unsteady, but Noah is quick to catch me. His hands cup either side of my ribs. I am super aware of how close they are to my breasts. They tingle with the closeness, and my face flushes.

"You right, Roberts?" he grins.

I nod, collect myself and head downstairs. I use the downstairs bathroom as Noah makes his way into the kitchen. I can hear him and Mum chatting away, and it brings a smile to my face. He really is good with adults. I am not. I always feel like a child on the brink of being in trouble.

As I return to the kitchen, I see that Noah has stayed true to his word and has fetched my sketch pad from under the sink and is looking through it. Mum just looks at me with a knowing smile on her face. I think it's a smile of approval. Not that I need it. There's nothing to approve. We're just friends.

"Your father would love to see his beloved darling daughter in this state," she jokes.

"Where is Dad?" I clear my throat.

"He got called into work." Noah and I steal a concerned look at each other. "I'm catching up with the girls for our annual New Year's long lunch. I'll grab some take away on the way home. The boys want pizza. Is that ok with you?"

I nod. The thought of greasy food makes my stomach flip. I'm never drinking again.

"Noah, will you be staying for dinner?" Mum asks. I think she's a little sweet on Noah. Honestly, who isn't?

Noah says yes. Dinner seems like forever away, so I'm surprised he commits himself to spending that much time with me. He must really like pizza. Mum asks him what pizza he wants, and he replies with "Whatever you get is fine. I'll eat anything."

Mum smiles, satisfied with his answer. Elliott was always such a picky eater that it was easier when he didn't eat with us. I often went to his house for dinner just to avoid feeling awkward as he and Mum tried to work out a suitable meal option.

Mum excuses herself and leaves while I make vegemite toasties for Noah and me.

"The meal of champions," Noah states as we move to the lounge room and slump on the couch to flick through Netflix. We settle on some comedy movie that neither of us has any real intention of watching; it is purely background noise.

"So, what happened last night, Roberts?"

We keep our voices low. I tell Noah about how it looked like *The Plan* was working and then how I overheard Dad in the study. I tell him exactly what I heard and we both agree that he had to be talking to Miss Glossy Hair.

"What's the plan now, Roberts?"

I shrug my shoulders. "I can't say anything to him here. I literally vomited when he spoke to me."

Noah laughs. "Right."

"It's not funny. Confrontation makes me sick. I don't know, maybe I should go up there and try and catch them again. That way I don't have to say anything. If I catch them in the act and he sees me, then he'll have to talk."

"So, we're gonna follow him again?"

"We?" I smile.

"Don't think you're cutting me out now, Roberts. I'm too invested in this to be benched in the final play."

God, I want to kiss him. I want to climb in his lap and kiss him, but I can't be sure I won't throw up with any sudden movement.

"Alright, you're in."

"Thanks, coach." He salutes me.

"I need a driver anyway."

"Oh! Oh! So that's all I am to you, huh?" he mocks offense.

I put my hand to his head and pull a wayward strand of hair off his face. "But you're a really good driver," I tease.

He laughs again. "Right." Putting his plate on the coffee table, Noah jumps to his knees on the couch. He pulls me underneath him and begins tickling me. "Just a driver, huh?"

Through fits of laugher, I beg him to stop but he continues, becoming wilder as I laugh harder. He stands up and lets out a wild caveman roar before picking me up and slinging me over his shoulder. His show of strength weakens me further. He could be marching me to the pits of hell right now, and I wouldn't even care.

"Where are you taking me?" I say crying with laughter.

He doesn't respond except for cheekily slapping my behind. I continue to half-heartedly protest. I mean, I'm not really that mad at being somewhat in his arms. It's not until I realise that he has taken me out the back, that I kick up my protests. Literally.

"Noah, not the pool." I grab at his t-shirt, lifting up the back and grabbing at his skin. There is not an ounce of fat on the guy to grab. I run my nails over the small of his back hoping to tickle him. He lets out a pleased little whimper, so I do it again, realising I like being the cause of the noise coming from him.

"Say it," he teases.

"Say what?"

"That I'm more than just a driver to you." He is still joking but getting closer to the edge of the pool.

"Okay! Okay! You're more than just a driver. You're my baby daddy too."

He lets out a roaring laugh, and I squeal as he jumps into the pool with me still hanging over his shoulder. The fresh water stings as I come up gasping for air. He comes up chuckling, running his fingers through his long locks.

"That'll get rid of your hangover."

I splash him and swim to the edge of the pool. He follows, and we pull ourselves out of the water. I place my arms across my chest to cover myself. My t-shirt has gone see-through, and I'm not wearing a bra. Perfect. Realising what has happened, Noah flashes me that mischievous grin of his before taking off his wet t-shirt and wringing out the water. He hands it to me and tells me to put it on. I thank him, and he shrugs like it is no big deal.

We enter the house through the laundry where I know there are fresh towels. We stand there together drying ourselves off and seeing as though he is shirtless and in very close proximity to me, I decide now is as good a time as any to ask about his tattoo. At least it's a good distraction to the less than wholesome thoughts running through my head.

"Did they hurt?" I motion towards his chest.

"A bit. You kinda get used to it."

I point to the script under his arm. "What does that say?"

He lifts up his arm so I can get a better look at the ink against his brown skin. I unintentionally reach out to touch it and feel him shiver at my touch.

"Our destiny is no more in the stars than it is in our DNA," he recites.

"What does it mean? Is it like a famous quote or something?" I inquire.

"My pa said it. I think I need another toastie." He shuts down any further line of questioning.

I want to know more. We've been so caught up in my family drama that he's never mentioned his own family; or anything about himself for that matter. I want to ask more, I want to know more about him, but I sense that it is a topic that is closed to further discussions.

NINE

It's not long into the New Year when the perfect opportunity to follow my dad presents itself. I overhear Mum trying to plan a family day trip when my Dad apologises saying he can't make it and has to work. She questions him saying he has a lot of work on lately, and my heart races. Does she suspect there is something going on? I assumed that because I was blindsided by this that she was too, but maybe she has her own suspicions. I can't test that theory without giving everything away, though. Dad soothes her worries by claiming that they are down a doctor at work because one of his colleagues has a family emergency overseas, saying it's just an unusually busy time of year for babies to be born.

"You can never predict when they'll come." It is Dad's favourite saying. It is really grating on me this time though.

Still, I knew this is an opportunity, so I text Noah and he agrees to meet me before my dad leaves in the morning so we can follow him. I tell Mum I am going out on a road trip with Noah for the day, and that we are leaving early so I won't be here when she wakes up. It is easier to keep up with my own lies if they're only half lies.

I meet Noah a little further down the street and climb into his car. I've packed some chocolate biscuits and other snacks for our trip. He dives into the bag of goodies as soon as I hop in the passenger seat.

"Hey! They're meant to last us the whole day," I say, swatting his hand away.

"Why are you dressed like that anyway?"

I think what I've chosen to wear is perfect for the day; black leggings, black long-sleeve top and black boots. Ninja style. Spy style. "We're on a stakeout. How am I supposed to dress?"

"Like it's gonna be thirty-six fucking degrees and not like you're off to the snow."

"Okay, well that's an exaggeration. If I was going to the snow, I'd have brought a jacket." I wave my hand dismissively at him and focus on the road ahead, waiting for Dad's car to come past us.

I really should have checked the weather forecast though. If it is going to be thirty-six degrees today, then I am going to roast. At least we'll be inside Noah's car with the air conditioning for most of the day, right?

Just before 6.30am, Dad's car drives past us, and Noah slowly pulls out to follow him. Noah let's a couple of cars get ahead to once again hide us. As we leave the green openness of the peninsula for the concrete barriers of the freeway, I find myself feeling claustrophobic.

The high rises of the Melbourne skyline come into focus, and it feels like stepping into a different realm. We turn off at Batman Avenue and drive through Melbourne's sporting precinct. The grandness of the large football stadiums and Melbourne Park which surround us remind me of just how small we are. Dad drives through the city and saves us from another hook turn by taking a back street through to the apartment blocks from the other day.

Noah and I share a worrying glance; his is concern for me and mine is also concern for me. It's a strange feeling to catch someone doing something you know they're not supposed to. Part of me is happy that I've caught him out again, as if it confirms I'm not crazy; but the other part of me is sad and disappointed that this is happening at all.

Noah and I don't say anything while we wait, parked in the street. We'd both make terrible spies because Noah has already made his way through all of the snacks, and I didn't think of things like bathroom breaks; where exactly would we go, and how would we divide it up? What happens if Dad suddenly appears and we have to quickly follow him but one of us is in the loo? Speaking of which, I really need to go.

"I really need to pee," I blurt out.

"Didn't you go before we left?"

"I did, *Dad*," I tease, "but that was over an hour ago. It's okay for you, you can just go on any tree."

He laughs. "And get slapped with a public urination fine." He shakes his head at a memory, and I remind myself to ask him about it later. "Can you hold it?"

I nod. I sure hope so. Hopefully they're not going to be too long. I try and think of something other than my suddenly very full bladder, but every thought keeps coming back to water.

"Noah, I don't think—"

"Shhh," he interrupts and points out the front window.

There they are, Dad and Miss Glossy Hair, only this time they aren't alone. They have two small children with them. A boy and a girl. The boy looks the oldest, maybe four, and the girl looks like she has just begun walking. She has a dummy in her mouth and a soft teddy in her hands. She's a little wonky on her feet. Dad has changed his outfit too. Gone is his grey suit and checked shirt, replaced by chino shorts and a collared t-shirt, classic Dad uniform. So, he has a change of clothes at her place, and she has children. He is busy taking her children out for the day instead of spending time with his own family. I scrunch my hands into a fist.

"Arsehole," Noah mumbles as he pulls out to follow the car.

I don't correct him. I don't scold him for talking about my dad that way because I agree with him. On the drive up, I told Noah about Mum's attempt at planning some family time together only for Dad to knock her back. Seeing this is a huge kick in the guts.

Not knowing the city very well, I have no idea we're heading to the zoo until we get there. We haven't been to the zoo in years, not since the twins were babies. Dad was always too busy, and Mum said she couldn't handle all three of us on her own. Noah and I stand a good distance back, always ensuring we can see where Dad is, but he can't see us.

Noah, always the gentleman, pays for our entry tickets as I keep eyes on Dad. We follow them along the bamboo-lined elephant trail, which is littered with families and provides plenty of cover. For me, anyway. Noah's height and his biker meets rock star looks make him stand out from the crowd. Today, he wears his hair up, and his usual uniform of board shorts and a tank top shows off his impressive muscle. His wrists are covered with an assortment of leather bracelets and today, he wears three piercings along his left ear. It works for us that Dad hasn't met Noah yet, so to him, Noah is just another face in the crowd. A handsome face. I just have to make sure I hide behind him so that I'm not seen. I pull Chris' plain black baseball cap from my bag and tuck all of my hair into it. Bits dangle around my face as I have too much hair for the cap.

I notice the way other girls, and women, look at Noah. I'm not blind. Girls with their families look at Noah with side eyes, girls with their friends are obvious in their looking and giggling. Women do the double take thing and pretend to be looking at something beyond him. I feel embarrassed for them and myself too; I can only imagine what they're saying about me. I am not worthy. Noah doesn't notice, or if he does, I can't tell. He is humble. It is a different feeling than being with Elliott. The girls would all stare at him too, but he'd walk around with his chest puffed out and an air of arrogance about him. I mistakenly took that for confidence at one point. I know better now.

As we are following Dad, the little boy backtracks and runs in our direction.

"Shit," Noah says under his breath.

We are surrounded by families and boxed in by prams; we can't make a quick getaway. Dad chases after the runaway, and my heart races so fast, I feel like it's going to burst through my chest. He is going to see us.

"Don't kick me in the nuts." Noah grabs me by the waist, pulls me in and begins kissing me. Slow and soft. I disappear into his hulking arms and into the moment. No one else exists but us. I have no idea where Dad has gone, or if the child has been collected, and I don't care. I run my hands up his firm arms, his shoulders and finally around his neck. His coarse beard tickles my chin. He pulls me in closer, pressing hard up against my body. All too soon he breaks away, his hands staying put around my waist. He looks around. "All clear."

I'm anything but! My mind is completely hazy, and I'm totally disorientated. He lets me go and turns in the direction we were originally heading. He doesn't say anything further and neither do I. Even if I wanted to, I can't! I have never been kissed like that. Elliott *never* kissed me like that. I want Noah to kiss me again and again, but I don't know if he wants to. He seemed into it in the moment, but the moment has passed. He's said before he doesn't think kissing is a big deal, but how can a kiss like that not be a big deal?

I'm still trying to catch my breath as we walk towards the second elephant enclosure and get stuck in a shady corner. Noah quietly moves me to the wall and stands in front of me, facing me with his fingers to his lips. I nod and rest my hands on his torso. Firm. Unlike my legs which have turned to jelly. He puts his arms around me but is looking over his shoulder. I can hear them come forward, Dad's voice first. He's telling them some obscure fact about elephants which I figure is for the benefit of Miss Glossy Hair more so than the kids. My body begins to shake like I'm cold which makes Noah hold me tighter.

"This is so nice Andy," I hear Miss Glossy Hair say.

I look up at Noah and poke my tongue out in disgust and mouth *Andy?* Noah gives me a wry smile. Dad has never been an "Andy". Noah and I continue to look at each other as we listen to their conversation. I hadn't noticed the small flecks of amber in his brown eyes until now. They are hypnotic.

"I'm glad you could get away," Miss Glossy Hair says and my fists clench, "it's so nice to have this time together." I hear them kiss. I'm sure steam escapes my ears.

"Daddy!"

I freeze. Noah holds me as tight as he can, afraid that if he doesn't, I might crack into a thousand pieces. We look at each other, eyes wide in shock.

"Daddy! Daddy! Daddy!"

"Yes buddy, I'm right here."

I don't see, but I imagine that he scoops the kid up into his arms because the kid stops calling out for him and begins to giggle.

"I want to see lions now!"

"Okay, buddy, let's go see them. Roar!"

We don't follow them. I can't. I'm frozen to the spot where my world just imploded. This problem has morphed into a living, breathing, inescapable nightmare. Dad isn't just having an affair; he has a whole other family! I let the thought sink in, and I wonder what that means for us. Were we not good enough for him? Does he not love us anymore? Is that why he ran off and started a family with someone else?

Noah and I don't move, he doesn't let me go, and I somehow know he won't until I give him a sign that it is okay to do so. I don't think it will ever be okay. People move around us, noise fills the space, but I feel like I'm stuck watching it all happen again in slow motion.

"I want to go home." It's barely louder than a whisper, but it is enough for Noah to spring into action.

TEN

We don't speak on the ride home. Noah doesn't ask me what *The Plan* is now, and he doesn't tell me what a complete and utter arsehole my father is. He doesn't ask me if I am okay because he can see that I'm not. The only noise we drive to is the sound of the radio. When we finally make it home, I don't invite Noah in, but he follows me anyway, somehow knowing that is exactly what I want him to do. I don't want him to leave, but I can't bring myself to talk. I can hear the twins are outside in the pool. Mum has made herself comfortable on the couch, catching up on her shows. She calls out to us that there are snacks in the fridge and to help ourselves. All this noise around me of a normal, functioning family home is muted and muffled as though I'm experiencing it all underwater.

Drowning.

I tell Noah that I'm going to change and that I will meet him by the pool. He waits and watches me as I head upstairs, probably contemplating whether or not to follow me. He doesn't, and I retreat to my room, past the happy family photographs that hang on the walls. They're like a dagger to my heart. They're a lie. My life is a lie. I close my bedroom door and peel off my clothes as if on automatic pilot. I change into my navy and gold bikini and just stand in the middle of my room. The first tear rolls down my cheek, followed by another. My whole body is shaking as I sob and drop to my knees on the bedroom floor.

My door opens, and I see Noah. His expression is pained. He sees me on the floor and quickly turns to shut the door behind him. He slides over and scoops me up into his lap. I throw my arms around his neck and cry into his shirt. He rubs my back and gently rocks us back and forth, soothing me. I lose time in his arms.

When I come around, I pull myself ever so slightly away from him, and the mess I made on his shirt. I stay in his lap and he uses his thumb to wipe away the remainder of my tears.

"Sorry I snotted all over your top." We both let out a little laugh.

"Don't worry about it." He kisses my forehead.

I sniff. "How could he do that to us?"

Noah shakes his head. "I don't know, Chels."

I smile at him. It's the first time I've heard him use my name, and it feels like melted chocolate; smooth, warm and delicious. I lean in and softly kiss his lips.

"Thank you." I whisper in between kisses.

"For what?" He searches my face.

"For just being here."

He pulls me in, his kiss more urgent. His hands move around my body, slowly, tenderly exploring. I mirror his movements and unfurl my legs, one around each side of his hips. I slowly move into him, and he lets out a low groan. I should stop this now before it goes any further, but I can't. My body moves in sync with his. A knock at the door followed by someone barging in immediately stops us.

"Eww! Gross."

"Cody!" I yell.

Noah instinctively swings us around to shield me from my brother. Although I'm still in my bathers and he's in his clothes, watching your sister straddle a guy in her bedroom is not a pretty sight.

"Knock, then wait to be let in!"

"Yuck!" Cody pokes his tongue out.

"What do you want, little perv?" Noah's impatient.

"Mum wants you downstairs. She's organising dinner." He puts his finger in his mouth and makes vomit noises as he exits the room.

Noah chuckles, and I bury my head in his chest. "Well, that was scarring."

"Hey, at least we still had our clothes on. Five minutes later, and it would have been another story."

I instinctively know I turn a deep, deep red. I kiss him again quickly before standing up. "I suppose we better get down there."

Noah stays seated on the bedroom floor. "Yeah, you're gonna have to give me a minute." He flashes me that cheeky grin of his and watches me throw a dress over my bikini. "Normally I'd protest about you wearing more clothes, but I like that dress on you."

It is my sunflower dress. I've worn it more in the last two weeks than I have in the last two years. It has always been my favourite dress, and I'd forgotten how good I felt in it. Maybe I just like the way Noah looks at me in it; like I'm a beautiful painting.

"Should I just meet you down there?" I offer.

"Probably best. You're not really helping the situation." He winks at me.

I lean down and give him one last kiss before I head downstairs to see what Mum wants. I'm a little short with her for ruining my time with Noah. All I want to do is go back up there and be with him.

"Your brothers ate the leftovers for lunch, and I cannot be bothered to cook today. So, I'm doing take-away." She presents multiple menus to me like a prize on a game show.

"Whatever you want, Mum."

"You say that, but then I get something, and someone always whines. Ah, Noah."

Noah arrives and stands behind me, placing his arms around my waist and briefly kisses my shoulder. I think I might become a permanent shade of red around him. I look sheepishly at Mum for a reaction, but she doesn't give one. I feel a little awkward with PDA in her presence but she's playing it very cool.

"Noah, what take-away do you want? And don't say 'whatever' like this one." She points at me.

He picks up a few different menus and looks them over. I know he won't care what we eat, but Mum has thrown him a challenge, and he must pick something.

"Thai?" I suggest.

"Yep. Sounds good to me." He places the menu back down and looks for approval from Mum.

She ums and ahs before saying that she doesn't really feel like Thai. We go back and forth like this until Dad suddenly appears wearing his grey suit and checked shirt. Very cunning. He kisses Mum on the forehead, and I feel sick thinking back to him kissing Miss Glossy Hair at the zoo. He's like a snake, slipping between the cracks of two different worlds. My whole body feels unsteady.

"Hello, love."

"Hi, how was your day at work?"

I grab hold of Noah's top and scrunch it into a ball.

"Good love, busy. Hi," he looks to Noah and extends his hand, "Andrew Roberts."

Noah graciously takes it. "Noah Kalani."

I glare at my father. There is no recognition of the man I know. Just a stranger and a liar standing before me. A cheat. Rage fills my body. I feel hot.

"Glad you're home. We are just deciding what to have–"

"Actually," I cut her off, "Noah and I are going out." I grab his hand and start to turn.

"Well hang on, Chelsea," Dad says, and I hate that I stop for him, "I want to tell you something before you go."

I squeeze Noah's hand. This is it. He's going to confess his sins over take-away menus. We'll never be able to eat take-away again.

"I've managed to get the next couple of days off work, and I'm not on call, so we're going to go and visit Grandpa and Nanna. As a family." He looks directly at me with that last part.

I can't help but let my disappointment show. *Coward.*

"But we just saw them at Christmas!" I protest.

I love my grandparents, but I am angry that he doesn't confess.

"Yes Chelsea, *you* did. *I* didn't. *I* was working. Now that I have a few days off, I'd like us to be together as a family." His words are stern.

Which family?

I shake my head. "No."

"Excuse me?"

"I don't want to go with you."

"Excuse me, young lady, you are not too old to be reprimanded for your behaviour."

"Chelsea, come on honey, we've been trying to get away as a family all holidays and finally Dad has some time." Mum pleads.

"We're going." I storm out leading Noah to the front door.

He's respectful, so he says a short goodbye. I can hear Dad call out to me, and Mum telling him to let me go. I don't turn around and head straight for Noah's car.

"Where to, Roberts?"

"Anywhere but here."

ELEVEN

Noah drives to a secluded back beach further along the peninsula that I have never been to before. It's a strange contrast to the green rolling hills of the wineries all around us, in the middle of what seems like the country, there are kilometres of sand and ocean. He says it's his secret surf spot which explains why I've never heard of it. It may surprise some people, but not all of us who grow up along the sandy beaches of the peninsula like to surf. Give me a pool any day. Today though, the beach is the perfect spot. We walk down to the sand dunes and open the fish and chips we picked up on the way. I pick at the food, not really that hungry. We share a bottle of water and have the beach to ourselves. The light is beginning to fade, and the seagulls circle us, intent on stealing our food. My phone buzzes with a message from Mum. She writes a long message about how good some family time would be and that a couple of days away from Noah won't be that bad. I scoff. She thinks I don't want to go away because I don't want to be away from Noah! She's so naïve and foolish, how could she be so blind? It makes me so mad. Noah asks me about the message, and I show him.

"*You'll be fine without Noah for two days. I'm sure he'll wait for you,*" he reads the message out loud. "Sounds like you're going to war, Roberts."

"More like hell."

My phone buzzes again. It's Mum. My curfew is 10pm sharp. The punishment for my outburst. I put my phone on silent and stuff it back into my pocket.

"I don't know how I can go away with him for two days; I can't even stand to be in the same room as him for two minutes!"

"If it gets too much just text me, and I'll come get you." Noah offers like it's no big deal.

"It's like, a four-hour drive! I can't ask you to do that."

He shrugs. "It's not like I have anything better to do, remember, I'm just waiting for you," he jokes, and I smile.

He always makes me smile. My anger melts away.

"Seriously though, it's no biggie."

"Thank you." I want to kiss him, but I've lost my nerve.

We watch the waves crash ashore together in silence, and it's comfortable. I don't feel the need to fill the silence. I gather my thoughts. Two days away with my family is a lot to take at the best of times, let alone when two of us are holding onto a massive secret. There aren't as many places to hide at Nanna and Grandpa's house and the focus will be on doing things together as a family, just like I saw him do today with his newer, younger family. How can I possibly keep this to myself? How can he?

"Noah, do you think I should tell Mum?"

He shakes his head. "I don't think she'll believe you. I think he needs to tell her. He messed up, he has to own up."

Tears roll silently down my cheeks. This doesn't happen to our family; this happens to other people's family. I've never felt so alone in my life and yet I have Noah here, and he makes me feel so secure, cared for. He makes it less lonely, and I know that makes no sense whatsoever, but that's how I feel; like I'm swinging from one extreme emotion to another.

"Hey, hey, Chels." Noah moves to sit behind me, wrapping his arms around me.

"Sorry. I…I just don't know what to do. I don't feel like I know anything anymore. I mean, I looked up to my dad. I thought my parents had the perfect marriage. I *wanted* a marriage like theirs when I was older," I sniff and wipe away the tears with the back of my hand, "now none of it's real, you know?"

"I know. It's fucked up. But hey, you're still you—"

"But who am I if everything has changed? If my family's not what it seems, then who am I?"

We've always been a close family, or so I thought. Every decision I've ever made has been made with Mum and Dad's guidance because I believed they knew what was best for me. I believed they made all the right decisions in life to end up where they were, and I wanted to be just like them. I wanted to have a long lasting, happy marriage to a man that loved and adored me even with all the challenges life throws your way. I modelled myself and my life on theirs because I thought they were everything I wanted to be, and now I've discovered it's all just a lie. I couldn't make Elliott stay with me. Mum couldn't keep Dad from straying, and things with Noah will probably be over before they really start.

Nothing is forever.

Especially love.

What is the point of any of it?

"You know my tattoo?" Noah interrupts my thoughts.

I turn to face him, confused about what this had to do with my world collapsing around me. I nod, *our destiny is no more in the stars than in our DNA*. I have memorised it.

"A couple of years ago I went through some shit like you are now. I found out my dad wasn't my real dad," he pauses, pained by the memory. My breath catches in my throat. I hug one of his arms to show my support as he continues. "He didn't know either. It was a shock to both of us. Turns out she had an affair with someone from work. I kept that secret out of shame. I was ashamed of my mother, and I felt shame for my father. I also felt shame for being some bastard kid." He clears his throat. "Made me mad, got me into a lot of trouble, especially at school, broke my family apart. I moved in with my nan and pa. It was Pa who told me that I am me. I'm not my parents or whatever anyone else thinks of me. I am me, and I have the power to be whoever I want to be. My story hasn't been written yet. Shit things happen, but they're not me. It's how I react to them that defines who I am."

I cock my head to the side. "But you have no control over the things that happen to you. That's destiny. You're saying you're in control of that."

"You're in control of how you respond to it. When shit things happen, you have two options; sink with it and let it affect you or accept it and move past it. It's like with your old man, it's a shit thing, right?"

I nod. "A very shit thing."

"Totally. No one is denying that. But you can either let it affect you and your relationships with your mum, your brothers, boyfriends – whatever, because you now believe all men are dirty, lying scumbags," he checks for understanding and I nod, "or, you acknowledge that he's the scumbag, cheat and liar and the rest of us dudes aren't all that bad. Just 'cause he messed up doesn't mean your life if going to be. That's how you create your own destiny."

Behind the wild hair and tattoos, Noah is an old soul. I'm floored by his revelations and don't know how to respond. I can only imagine what he must have gone through. I'm navigating a fractured family – his was torn apart. I wish I'd known when we were at school together. I wish we'd been friends then. I could have comforted him, helped him through it like he is helping me now.

"That shit will cost you 170 bucks an hour, once a week for three years." Noah's joke breaks the heavy mood.

We laugh and share a smile. "So, do I pay now or later?"

"It's alright, Roberts, for you, I'll give you anything you want for free." He leans down and kisses me. "You know, I've never told anyone any of that. About my family."

I smile and bring my hand to his face, rubbing his cheek. I have been so desperate to know more about him. I didn't expect to find out we share a similar heartbreak. I feel safe in his arms and in his trust.

"Have you met your real dad? Your biological one I mean?"

Noah shakes his head. "He died when I was a baby. Car accident."

"I'm so sorry." I wrap my arms around him, wanting to take away his pain.

He lets out a sigh. "Enough of the heavy shit."

I give him my best oh-please eyes. "It's actually nice to talk about something other than my family for a change."

"Swap one screwed up situation for another."

"We're more similar than I realised." I begin drawing in the sand with my fingers.

Noah's hands join in, and we make patterns around us.

"Right, your turn."

I look at him confused. "My turn for what?"

"Tell me something."

"You already know my something."

He smiles. "Something else."

Something else. Do I have anything else? I think, pushing aside my mess, searching for something else. Nothing else seems important right now. "I don't want to do journalism. It's my first preference on my VTAC form, but I really don't want to do it. I want to do art."

It seems insignificant right now, but it's something. Year 12 seems so long ago, and uni seems too far away. With everything else that is happening, uni seems like it belongs in someone else's life, not mine.

"Then do it," he says simply.

I laugh. "I can't! My parents would never approve. Art is okay for a hobby but not a career in their eyes."

"Who cares what they think. Do what *you* want."

"I haven't told anyone that yet."

I haven't even really told myself that yet. My parents know that I didn't get the score needed for a medical career although it didn't stop Dad from trying to find a way in for me. I had a weird sense of relief when my ATAR came in. I must have been the only Year 12 student in the whole of the country who was hoping their ATAR wasn't high. I applied for a range of things; things that sounded okay during my interview with the careers' counsellor at school. Everyone – my parents, the counsellor - had agreed that I was "too smart" to waste my time doing something as "frivolous as the arts" (Dad's words). They didn't value it like I did. I didn't want the confrontation or to face their disappointment, so I applied for anything outside of what I really wanted to do. Journalism seemed like a good compromise at the time – creative yet respectable. My heart's not in it though. I mean, I'm still not exactly sure what I want to do but who does at my age? It's a tonne of pressure for a seventeen-year-old to decide her life's path before she's even lived. I ask Noah if he felt the same when he finished school.

"I just did what made me happy. Hated school. The thought of doing more study made me want to jump off a bridge, so I just started up my own thing." He threads his fingers through mine. "You don't always have to go to uni, you know. You can do it your own way, if that's what you want."

This isn't an option for me. I've never been allowed to entertain the thought of not going to university like Noah or having a gap year like Willow; it isn't the Robert's Family Plan. I envy the freedom Noah has to chase his dreams his way.

"I've always wanted pink hair too," I add, changing the subject.

Noah smiles. "Hot, Roberts. Very hot."

It feels good to talk about what I want for a change. I haven't heard my own voice in a long time. I kiss Noah. Out here on the beach there is no one to interrupt us. It feels good to be in his embrace. I feel safe. I feel closer to Noah than I ever did to Elliott; than I ever have to anyone. Right now, Noah feels like the closest person to me in my life. Maybe it's because he shares in the biggest secret I've ever had to keep; or maybe it's something more.

TWELVE

Despite my protests, Noah has me back home minutes before curfew which undoubtedly pleases my parents. However, I wouldn't know because I storm past them on the couch and head straight to my room. I continue my silent treatment well into the morning and on the car ride to Nanna and Grandpa's house. I plug into my music to drown out the mindless chatter in the car. As I stare out the window, it seems that every second car is a Jeep like Noah's. At first, I thought – I hoped – it was him following us, ready to save me at any given moment. But as I spot more of them and in different colours, I realise it is nothing more than a cruel reminder of how long these next two days are going to feel without him.

Things have only just changed between us and I'm still not sure where we stand. I am very inexperienced at the whole dating thing as Elliott was my one and only boyfriend. Our relationship took a more traditional path; we'd been friends for years first before he asked me on a proper date to the movies and then kissed me at the end of the night. He told me he liked me and asked me to be his girlfriend. It followed clearly defined stages of relationship building.

All this stuff with Noah – the touches, the flirting, the kissing – are all amazing but we haven't had an official date (I don't call stalking my father a date). He's a very relaxed guy, and I worry that this attitude extends to his dating life. Casual and unattached. I don't think I could do that, not with him and how quickly I'm falling for him. And I totally am falling for him. I'm seeing his car everywhere; if that's not a sign I'm in deep then I don't know what is!

I just don't know how he feels. I can't ask him outright where we stand; it would make me seem so childish and high schooler. Urgh! And he's more mature than me, even if he is barely two years older. Maybe this is how real, adult relationships start, or don't start. It's all too confusing. Perhaps some time away will give me the thinking space I need. I mean, I like what he said about us being our own masters of our own destiny and all, but I'm still a huge believer in fate, and fate brought us together for a reason that day at the hospital. I just need to figure out what that is.

By the time we reach our grandparent's place down the winding roads of the Great Ocean Road, it is lunchtime, and I have stabbing pains in my stomach. I curse myself for not eating breakfast and hope that Nanna has baked something fresh to dive into. We stand around in the driveway of their beach house kissing and hugging hello before Nanna announces that she's made fresh banana bread and we should all come inside. Bless Nanna. I make my way in first, dumping my bags at the door and heading straight into the kitchen.

Nanna's banana bread is to die for and if I don't get there first, the twins will eat it all. I can tell Dad desperately wants to tell us off and lecture us about being gracious guests and having good manners– something about dumping our bags at the front door would feature heavily – but he knows better than to do that at Nanna's house. She'd have him put back in his place in ten seconds flat. Nanna's house, Nanna's rules. She is far easier going than my father. She'd love Noah.

"Right, I have fresh rolls and a hot chook for lunch. Once you're all done, we're headed to the beach for a bit of beach cricket and a nice walk." Nanna snaps into action and prepares lunch.

"Mum, it's been a long drive. I just want to relax," Dad pleads.

"Oh, nonsense, Andrew, all the more reason to get out into the fresh air. It's a beautiful day. You'll sleep well tonight."

And just like that he is a child again. He knows that arguing with Nanna is a waste of time, so he gives in and does as she says. I guess living a double life can make one tired.

Grandpa asks the boys if they have been watching the cricket and the four of them go on forever about the game. I seriously find it difficult to understand how there is *that much* to talk about with cricket. That and golf are the two most boring sports in the entire world. Nanna rolls her eyes; seems like she's had enough of the cricket season too.

"So Chelsea my love, what have you been up to?"

Oh, nothing much Nanna, making out with hot guy and following around Dad and his secret family. How about you?
"Not much," I answer.

"Chelsea has a new boyfriend," Cody shouts over the top of the conversation.

I shoot him a death stare. The boy can't hear you ask him to pass the remote while you sit next to him on the couch but can hear a private conversation at the other end of the table whilst supposedly being a part of another conversation! He makes me so mad.

"Ohhh, a boyfriend." Nanna teases.

"Well, he's not—"

"He's a lovely kid. Very handsome," Mum interrupts and emphasises the last part.

"Is that the guy I met yesterday?" Dad hollers from the other end of the table, "I didn't know he was your boyfriend. I thought *maybe*…but he seems a little old for you Chelsea."

Everyone is now joining in on the conversation, and I can't get a word in.

"How old is he?" Grandpa is shocked.

"That's my girl," Nanna winks at me.

"He's not that much older. He graduated from the same school as Chels, just a couple of years ahead of her," Mum adds.

"A couple as in two or three? Or a couple as in five or six?" Dad.

"Two," Mum.

"That's nothing," Nanna.

"Well, you tell him that your grandpa was in the navy."

"He's got the most beautiful brown skin," Mum.

"What's his name?" Nanna.

"He's a big dude," Cody and Chris in sync.

I put my hands up to quieten everybody down. They all stop and finally let me talk. "His name is Noah, Nanna, and we're just friends."

Cody scoffs at my claim, and I shudder when I think back to what he walked in on. I threaten him with my eyes while Mum mouths the word *"beautiful"* and outlines a muscular figure to Nanna. They both giggle.

"He was two years above me in school. He's a really great guy, but we're just friends." *Who kiss.*

"You show me a picture of him, and we'll talk more on our walk." Nanna winks at me. "Alright everyone, plates in the sink, and let's hit the beach!"

For people in their seventies, my grandparents are quite fit. Grandpa has taken over as bowler, Chris as batsman, Cody as wicket keeper and Dad is playing in the field (perfect spot for him). Mum makes herself at home on the sand dunes cheering everyone on while Nanna takes me up the beach for a walk. Nanna and I have always gotten along well. She's like a naughty schoolgirl trapped inside an old woman's body. She's embraced her grey hair but refuses to cut it, instead leaving it long to fall around her waist. She wears no make-up these days, but she doesn't need it. She's a natural beauty. We enjoy walking barefoot along the sand, her arm linked with mine. Nanna doesn't bother with small talk. She gets straight to the point; another reason I think she'd really like Noah.

"So, tell me more about this boy. Show me a picture."

I reach for my phone and show her the picture we took on the beach last night. The glow of the low evening sun dances across our faces, and I'm smiling. Noah is sitting behind me with his defined arms wrapped around my shoulders, kissing the top of my head. His hair is up in a bun, just how I like it, and he looks just as handsome side on as he does in any other way you could view him. I've fallen hard and it's written all over my face.

"Oh my! Look at those arms!" Nanna and I giggle. "Oh, he's very handsome. Rugged. Sexy." I don't blush for some reason when I am around Nanna. "I like his aura, Chels. I can see you like him too."

I nod. "I do. I think I really like him, Nanna." It feels good to say it.

She links her hand in mine and taps it. "Then go for it. What have you got to lose?"

"Everything. What if he doesn't like me back? What if it doesn't work out?"

"Nonsense. Look at that picture. He likes you alright. And so what if it doesn't work out! At least you'll have one hell of an adventure." I look at the picture and my heart swells. Nanna adds, "Trust someone who has had a bit more life experience than you when I say just relax and have fun. Stop over thinking everything. Be young."

I wonder if that's the same advice she gave to Dad at my age. "You and Grandpa got married at nineteen," I point out to her.

"And it was the worst decision we ever made."

I stop walking and stare at her. She isn't joking. She's serious. She laughs at me like she didn't just shatter the ground we are walking on.

She sighs. "I'm going to tell you something, but I don't want you to tell your father that I told you, okay? Can you keep a secret, Chelsea?"

I nod, I've been really good at that lately. I hold my breath, unprepared for what she's about to say.

"Your Grandpa and I love each other very much, let's be clear on that from the start," I breathe a little, "but we were so young when we got married. Kids who knew nothing of the world, nothing of ourselves and nothing of anything really. We went through a rough patch early on, separating. Before I fell pregnant with your father, I went on a six-month trip with a group of friends to 'find myself' as they say. I met the most wonderful man, and he taught me a lot about myself and spirituality. We had wild fun. It was very…liberating."

I find myself captivated by her storytelling. It's like she's gone back to that place and I can feel the energy and sense of freedom she is talking about. I want that.

"Anyway, it only lasted a few weeks before our group moved on to the next country, but I saw the world through a new lens. I felt like I finally knew who I was. For the rest of our trip, I was able to learn and grow in ways I couldn't before because I had held back. I was trying to be the person everyone else wanted me to be. Of course, when I came home, I wanted to keep that energy alive, so I moved here and bought this house. Your Grandpa followed me, and we realised we loved each other very much. I told him if he wanted to be with me then these were the changes that needed to be made. I told him the sort of life I wanted, and he agreed to it. To all of it. And well, you know the rest."

I did. I knew they moved from the city to the beach house and that Grandpa renovated it himself while Nanna ran her holistic centre from their lounge room. It wasn't until my aunties were born that they ventured out and bought a place for Nanna to expand her business, and by then, my grandpa had earned a reputation as quite the renovator and went into building. Three beautiful babies and now a herd of grandchildren and they lived happily ever after.

"Wow, Nanna. I never knew any of this." I shake my head in disbelief.

"Well, it's not something we reminisce about around the Christmas table. It may have turned out fine, but it's still a painful part of our history. What I'm getting at, Chelsea, is don't lock yourself into anything too young. You've done the serious boyfriend thing, and now you've finished school, the world is your oyster. Go and explore, you know, the world, people, everything. It is very hard to do that when you've locked yourself in."

I thought of Dad. Is this what he is doing? Had he locked himself in too young with Mum?

"Why are you telling me this now?" I ask.

"Because I should have had this same conversation with my own children."

I whip my head around to her. Does she know?

"What do you mean?" I'm breathless, searching for answers.

"I see the same pattern in you that I saw in your father." I freeze. "He had to have a plan, and he had to have everything figured out right then and there. He had a plan for the plan!"

She knows, she has to know.

Nanna continues, "It worked out just fine for your father because he married your mother and they're very happy together." She doesn't know. My heart sinks a little. "But you're different, Chelsea, you're a lot like me. You need to let go and be free. All that structure works well for academic people like your father, but us creative types, we can't be restricted. We need to fly."

I text Noah later that night.

C: Do you know how many people drive cars like yours? I saw so many on the way here, I seriously thought you were following us and coming to rescue me #stalker #sos

I wait for a reply that doesn't come. I contemplate sending him another message, but I don't. I retreat to social media and see what everyone else is doing. I stop by Noah's page first. He's uploaded a stock picture of the sun setting over a field of sunflowers with the caption "Waiting…". My heart skips several beats, and I hover over the like button until it turns into a love heart. I look at the time stamp and notice he posted it just before we arrived at Nanna and Grandpa's house. Maybe Nanna is right about him; maybe he likes me just as much as I like him.

Willow has posted pictures of herself at the strawberry farm. Most of them are selfies or close ups of her food, but I notice in the background that her stepsisters have arrived. She refers to them as The Dragons which is probably being too kind. They blame Willow's mum for taking their father away and by default despise Willow. They make her life a living hell whenever they come to visit, but they're sly, so their dad doesn't know what really goes on. He's under the illusion that all of the girls get along well. Willow's mother knows differently but begs Willow not to say anything, to keep the peace until they leave. They never stay for long which is what gets Willow through these visits. When Dad's secret family is revealed – *if* they're revealed – I wonder if that's how our family will be. Will his other children grow up to resent us, like we're trying to take their father away from them, or will we resent them? Right now, I don't think I have any feelings about them at all; they're so small and innocent in all of this. I certainly have a lot of feelings about their mother, and none of them are good.

It's getting closer to bedtime, and I still haven't heard back from Noah. I check my messages again, and I see that he hasn't even read the message. I wonder what he could be doing that has him so distracted that he can't read and respond to my message. In the time I've known him, he usually replies to a message almost instantaneously. I try not to think about it and get some sleep. I tell myself that I will text Willow in the morning and check in on her.

By morning I still haven't heard from Noah and the read receipt is showing that he still hasn't read the message. I scan social media but know it's hopeless; he's not a poster like me and my friends. I see his sunflower post has received over a hundred likes, and I feel happy, almost as if those likes are approval from his friends although I have no idea if they know we've been spending time together. I scan a few of the comments, most say things like "*stunning*" and "*beautiful*". Someone asked what he's waiting for, and Zane McIntosh has left a crude joke. Turns out, he's not as sweet as Willow thinks he is. I make a mental note to bring it up with her when I get back; once, of course, I've told her about Noah and me. Not that there is an "*us*" to tell her about. I don't think. Noah hasn't responded to any of the comments on the picture. I shoot Willow a quick message like I promised myself I would.

C: Hey babe, strawberry farm looked fun! Save some for me when I get back. At Nanna and Grandpa's 'til tomorrow. Xo

She responds immediately. Thank goodness someone does.

W: Was fun. Learnt that strawberries do not keep you safe from dragons. Still on the hunt for their kryptonite. Miss you. Remember we're working this Thurs xo

I smack my hand against my head. I had forgotten all about work and the re-opening on Thursday. Willow and I have worked for Pete since we were legally allowed to, and he schedules us on the same shifts figuring at least one of us will remember and remind the other. So far, his plan has worked.

C: Yes! Thank you! Totally forgot. What time are we on?

W: 11am 'til close. I gotta go, another family outing. Beach day. Like kill me, I'm a red head! See you at work xox

C: *crying laughing emoji* have fun babe xo

As I enter the kitchen, I see that I'm the last one awake despite it still being rather early in the morning. As much as I love summer break, I can never sleep in because it is too light in the mornings. Damn Daylight Savings! The longer light at the end of summer days is pure heaven, but the early morning light through the curtains is the devil. In the kitchen, everyone says their morning greetings, and I sit down to Nanna's freshly made eggs and bacon. I don't know what she does to get the eggs so fluffy, but she's a culinary genius.

"Up for a trip on the boat today, Chelsea?" Grandpa asks.

I love the boat, especially when it's docked, we're going nowhere, and the water is like glass. Although he asked, I don't think it is really a question.

"Sure." *Famous last words, Chelsea.*

Grandpa says we won't be out all day as he has to call in on a job site. Despite being retired, he's never fully retired. A lot of tradesmen he worked with still call him up and ask his advice on site. Nanna is the same; she still oversees a lot of her business even though my Aunt Amy runs it now. Dad says the two of them would go crazy if they actually retired. I guess his answer to that was to give them two more grandchildren. My stomach flips at the thought of having to share my grandparents with two little strangers. I push my breakfast aside; I've suddenly lost my appetite.

I down a couple of seasick tablets before we leave, just in case. I know the boys will want to stop for a little bit of fishing, so I take my sketch pad and pencil to keep me occupied. The last few days I've felt the itch to create again. I've mainly been drawing sunflowers, like the ones on my favourite dress, and hands, soft but manly like Noah's.

Grandpa speeds around and my brothers and I take turns on the donut off the back of the boat. Mum takes videos and photos, and all the adults howl with laughter whenever one of us falls off. I last longer than I have before although it's probably more out of fear of falling out of my bikini top than improved skill and balance. As predicted, the boys stop and fish. Nanna throws a line in too and Mum continues to be "official memory recorder".

I take myself to the front of the boat (The stern? The bow? Why can't it just be called the front?) away from everyone else and sunbake. Thankfully the water is still and so is my stomach. I have no reception on my phone which means I don't know if Noah is yet to read and reply to my message. I decide to take a few selfies and flick through which one I'll send Noah when I get back on shore. I'm partial to the one of me lying on my stomach with the ocean in the background. My boobs are pushed slightly up making them look fuller than normal, and you can see the hump of my behind as the picture leads out to the water. I'm smiling in my oversized sunnies and have pushed all my hair to one side. It's sexy without being too revealing; there's an element of cutesy innocence to it. This is the one I'll send when I'm back in range. Surely, he'll reply to that.

The noise from the back of the boat suggests they've caught something, and I can hear Grandpa make one of his silly jokes about being able to eat tonight. We don't stay out too much longer as it starts to get rough, and I complain enough that, apparently, I scare away all the fish. By the time we're back, I can barely move without wanting to vomit, a shell of the girl in the picture I took earlier. No one is sympathetic towards me. I make it back to the house without revealing the contents of my stomach. That's a win. I head straight for the couch. My brothers join me and promptly fight over the television remote.

I scan my phone hoping to take my mind off my stomach and to drown out my brothers. Still no word from Noah. I send him the picture from the boat and wait. I start to fall asleep, hoping that a nap will cure my nausea.

THIRTEEN

I feel someone shaking my shoulders to rouse me out of my sleep. It's Dad. I grab the blanket that has been placed over me as I slept and pull it up around my chin.

"Dinner time, Chels," he smiles at me.

I nod and retreat from his touch. He looks at me confused. "You alright, love?"

I nod again. We're alone in the lounge room. This is my opportunity to say something.

"Dad," I say, and he focuses his attention on me, "if you know a secret about someone, but they don't know you know, and this secret could really hurt a lot of people, would you confront the person with the secret or tell the person who is going to get hurt?"

He thinks about his answer, probably trying to follow my convoluted question. I'm not sure I even understand what I asked.

"Confront the secret keeper. Get them to tell the truth."

Interesting. "What if they don't? Or won't? Would you go and tell the other person, the one who'll get hurt?"

"Well then, Chels, I'd say you shouldn't be getting caught up in other people's business."

Of course, he would say that. That's how he's managed to keep his secret for so long.

"Is everything okay? You know, between you and Noah? Or Willow?"

"Yes, everything is fine with me and Noah," I snap. "Wait, why Willow?"

Dad shrugs his shoulders. "Just haven't seen her around much lately." *YOU haven't been around much lately*, I want to shout. "Mum says Noah's been at the house a bit."

"So?"

"Jesus, Chelsea, don't get so bloody defensive! What has gotten into you lately? All I'm saying is, don't forget to spend time with your friends too. Dinner is on the table." And with that he storms off muttering something about not understanding teenage girls.

I reach for my phone. Still no reply from Noah. Against my better judgement, and probably fuelled by my anger towards my father, I upload the picture of me on the boat to my socials: no caption, just a sun and captain's hat emoji. I leave my phone on the couch and join everyone else for dinner.

I don't say anything at the table as I can hear my phone buzzing and pinging from the other room. Each time it does, my eyes dart towards the lounge room, desperate to see if one of those messages is from Noah. Nanna has a no-phones-at-the-table rule, and normally I'd switch it to silent, but I was distracted and forgot. Now it was behaving like an itch I couldn't scratch. Nanna and Grandpa delight in telling us stories from Dad's childhood over dinner, and I swear, every time my phone makes a noise, Nanna deliberately comes up with another tale to tell, just to drag this out for a bit longer. The twins are loving hearing all the mischief Dad got up to in his youth because now they have ammunition against him for the next time they get into trouble. I've heard all these stories before, and they have lost their effect on me. On other occasions, I remember thinking that these stories of mischief seemed like they were stories of a different person, not my dad. Dad was always so in control and serious, that I could never connect him with these stories Nanna told. Now, knowing what I know, I can see how the two connect.

When dinner is finally over, I race to the lounge and check my phone. Most of the noises were social media notifications; the picture I posted is getting a lot of attention. I read some of the comments from my friends, Elliott and Willow both send me a flame emoji, but nothing from Noah. I reply to the comments with emojis and try, unsuccessfully, not to think of Noah.

It isn't until I'm getting ready for bed that my phone buzzes, and I finally hear from Noah. I breathe a sigh of relief.

N: Alright Roberts you've got my attention. And everyone else's.

Was he mad? Clearly, he'd been looking at my socials to make a comment like that. He may not have commented but he is keeping tabs on me. I feel a little foolish.

C: So you are alive!

N: Sorry. Been busy.

C: What have you been up to?

Those damn three dots appear and then disappear without a message. I'm glued to my phone as if it holds all the secrets of how they built the pyramids. Nothing. More minutes pass, and I feel uneasy. There is a shift between us, and I can't figure out why.

N: Just stuff. Got 2 go. See ya tomoro when u get back

I don't bother responding. His texts seem cold. Short. Was he mad about me posting the picture to social media? Maybe he thought it was just for him, and it was, originally. Surely, he wouldn't get so worked up over something like that, not Noah. He was so carefree. I want to go home and see him, and figure this out. Something is off, and I want to know what it is.

FOURTEEN

The next morning, I am packed and ready to go before everyone else. I'm keen to get home and see Noah. This trip hasn't provided me with any space to think; things with Noah are more confused; I still can't stand my father; and I've just discovered the hidden family secret of Nanna's little adventure when she wasn't much older than me. I have Dad pushing me down the path of plans and structure, and Nanna and Noah encouraging me to break free and find my own path, and none of this even touches on what I should do regarding Dad's affair and secret family! Honestly, I feel like my world is spinning out of control. I want to get home and back on to what feels like solid ground. This trip has done nothing except make everything more complicated.

My phone buzzes with a text message from Willow. She's sent me a screenshot of a post on someone's Facebook page. It's a picture of Noah playfully scrunching up his face at the camera and poking his tongue out while a girl I don't recognise is lifted onto his back with her arms draped around his neck, biting his ear lobe. There's no caption other than a black love heart emoji. My phone buzzes again and it's a screenshot of some of the comments. I wish I hadn't read them. "*Yaaaaasssss*" reads one. "*You two are so cute together*" reads another and finally "*Best pic ever! Love you two xxx*". I can feel the tears welling up. My phone buzzes again.

W: WTF??!!!

My thoughts exactly, Will. I stare at my phone and then re-read the comments – self-punishment. I feel like the wind has been knocked out of me. Elliott. Dad. Noah. They're all the same. Jerks.

It's raining and cold by the time we get home which is typical of a Melbourne summer; you are melting one day and freezing the next. Willow has sent me a few more messages asking if I am alright. I don't text her back because I don't know if I am. I feel exhausted. I am exhausted from everything to do with my dad, exhausted from fighting with Elliott, and I am exhausted from trying to figure things out with Noah.

I am just done.

It's not supposed to be this complicated.

I spend the rest of the afternoon watching mindless TV and eating a packet of biscuits. Noah messages and asks if I am home. I ignore his message. Maybe if I ignore him long enough, he'll take a hint and slowly disappear from my life, and we can avoid talking about that picture. Nanna was wrong about him. I'm probably just one of many girls he's seeing, keeping things casual, the Noah way. I take myself to bed, and this time, I turn my phone off to shut out the world.

The next morning the sun is playing peek-a-boo with my curtains and wakes me up. I'm in no better a mood and feel sluggish and heavy. The weight of keeping these secrets and all this uncertainty is getting to me. I'm actually thankful to have work today as a distraction. Hopefully we will be busy enough that I can avoid talking about any of this with Willow on shift. I need my best friend now, but in a space where we can lay on a bed and eat spoonsful of ice cream straight from the tub. We've been unusually quiet with each other this summer, and I feel guilty for keeping all these secrets from her.

Mum seems extra bright this morning, probably because she's managed to fling the twins off to a friend's house and me at work, which means she has time to herself. I ask what she is going to be doing with all her free time today.

"I think I might go into the city and surprise your dad for lunch. I haven't done that in ages."

I freeze in my seat. This is bad. I should say something. Warn her. What if she sees him with Miss Glossy Hair? As much as I want her to know the truth (I think?), I don't want her to have to see it with her own eyes. No matter how many times I blink or wash them out in the shower, the image of Dad kissing another woman is burned into the very depths of my eyeballs. I see it whenever I close them. She doesn't need that.

"Do you think that's a good idea, Mum? He's probably busy." I try to sound casual, so I don't tip her off. "He wasn't there when I went up, remember?"

"No, it'll be fine. If he's busy, then I'll just do some shopping. Are you sure Willow's okay to drop you home tonight? If she's too tired to drive, I can come and get you both."

I need to stop Mum from going into the city and potentially having her heart broken. I can't think quickly enough of another excuse. *Think, Chelsea, think!*

"She'll be fine. Are you sure you want to go all the way into the city? Don't you just want to enjoy having the house to yourself and catch up on your shows? Or read in peace?"

She pulls into the parking lot at Pete's and kisses me on the cheek. "No, it'll be fun. Go on, get to work. Have a good shift, sweetie. Say hi to Willow for me."

I reluctantly get out of the car, and she drives off. I should have said something more to stop her from going into the city! I'm such an idiot. I can't work, not when the fate of my family is being decided while I serve pancakes and milkshakes to other happy families! Will I even have a family to come home to after my shift?

FIFTEEN

Pete has renovated the pancake parlour to look like a 1950s diner. Neon lights, car parts, jukeboxes at each booth and fifties memorabilia are scattered throughout the place. He's done a really good job. I feel like I've legit stepped back in time. As I walk through to the staff room, I can see it's going to be a busy shift as the restaurant is full already. In my locker hangs a new uniform; white blouse and a fifties style swing skirt with lots of tulle underneath. There's a picture hanging there too, the same one he sent us home with before Christmas. It explains how to wear my hair and make-up – fifties style. Looks like we're really embracing the whole theme.

We make it through the lunch time rush. Willow and I have no time to talk. None of us do. We pass pleasantries as we race to serve customers and tell Pete how great the place looks.

It's late afternoon by the time Willow and I are allowed to take our break. We only get half an hour now before the dinner rush and another break a little later when it quietens down. Willow grabs at my hands and drags me over to sit in the shade under our favourite tree. I brace myself for what's coming.

"So, have you spoken to him?"

I shake my head.

"Why not? Don't you want to know who she is? What's going on?" Willow demands.

I slouch in the seat and throw my head back. "I can't be bothered, Will. I have so much other stuff going on right now."

"Like what?"

I want to tell her, just not here.

"Family stuff. It doesn't matter." I hope it's enough of an explanation for her. I'm not in the mood to fend off any more questions. So I add, "It's not like anything happened between us anyway. I mean, we kissed but that's it."

But it felt intimate. It felt real. It felt special.

She claps her hands together. "I knew it! I knew it! See, now that you've kissed someone else, you can move on from Elliott. I'm sure this picture is nothing."

Elliott? What does any of this have to do with him? Why does she keep bringing him up when I'm trying to forget him? It's starting to bother me.

"You know, Chels, I think you should talk to him. Just sort it out. I mean, I saw the picture of you on the boat," she eyes me suspiciously, "that was the most un-Chelsea picture I've ever seen. And it was for him, yeah?"

Her words sting. I like that picture. I didn't know it was "un-me". What does that even mean? Maybe it is very *me*. Maybe it's the new me. The me whose family is breaking apart.

The me whose father has a secret family. She can't say it isn't *me* when I don't know who *me* is any more.

"Did it work? Did you get his attention? I mean, don't get me wrong, you looked totally hot. But it wasn't really you. I don't know, Chels. Things seem off with you."

I don't know what to say and even if I did know, I don't have the energy to get into it. Instead, I sit in silence and listen to my best friend roast me.

"I just think you should call him and ask about the photo. You'll be eighteen next month, Chels. We'll be hitting up all the clubs! It'll be easy to get over him if that's what this comes too. You just need to know, you know?"

Calling him would lead to confrontation, and I avoid confrontation. Even right now. Besides, calling him and talking about the photo is basically admitting that I like him, like *really* like him, and then what if he doesn't feel the same way? That's humiliation on a whole other level. I change the topic and ask about her stepsisters. She spends the rest of our break telling me all the mean and sly things they got up to while they were here. Luckily for Willow, they've gone back to their mother's house, The Dragon's Den, as Willow calls it, and she won't have to see them for at least another six months.

By the time our break is over, the restaurant is busy again with families and their young children coming in early for dinner. The place is soon buzzing with more and more people. Willow and I are taken off the floor and placed on drinks. Willow is eighteen which means she can serve the alcohol while I mix the shakes and any other non-alcoholic drinks. My feet hurt from running around on them all day and my lower back is joining the party.

At Pete's Pancake Parlour, patrons come up to the bar to order their drinks. People who pop in before heading out elsewhere for the evening take a seat at the bar and order drinks. We're cheaper than most of the pubs, so we get groups of people my age coming in for pre-drinks before a night out. Willow and I prefer working the bar; it's still busy but at least you get to talk to people. Tonight though, I don't feel like talking.

Sometime just after eight, Elliott and a group of friends from school walk in. As he approaches the bar, I see Noah enter the restaurant behind him. Dressed in ripped jeans, faded tank and with his hair down, he chats to one of the waiters and grabs a booth. He has come with a group of people too. He's scanning the restaurant for someone; me? How would he know I was working tonight? I notice the girl from the photograph makes up one of the members of Noah's group although they don't sit next to each other. Tommy and Zane are there too.

"Chelsea." There are fingers clicking in my face to get my attention. It's Elliott. "Earth to Chels, you here?"

"Yeah, sorry, hi." I shake myself back to the present.

I continue to make the orders as Elliott talks. "Listen, Chels, I just want to say I am sorry about the other night. I guess, I'm just—" he leans in closer over the bar, "I'm just having a hard time letting go of you."

I stare up at him and spill milk everywhere. Willow drops a glass behind me. I didn't know she was there. I grab a few rags and clean it up. Elliott leans over the bar top, trying to help. Willow cleans up the broken glass and scurries off to remake the order.

"Listen, I'm having a party tomorrow night. My place. Why don't you come, and we'll work at this whole being friends thing?" He smiles at me.

I can't keep up with Elliott's changing moods. His offer makes me dizzy. A large figure appears behind Elliott, one hand slaps him on the back, while the other takes a handful of nuts from the bowl on the bar. The figure takes a seat.

"Is this douche bothering you, Roberts?" Noah smiles at me and then gives a stern look towards Elliott.

I shake my head, wiping my hands on the apron. "No, it's fine."

Elliott takes this as his cue to leave. He looks uncomfortable in Noah's presence. "Just let me know, Chels. Willow's coming. It'll be fun."

"So much fun," Noah mocks as Elliott walks away. "What a dick."

"Do you know him?" I ask, annoyed.

"Harrowhill? Yeah, he got me suspended once. Caught me and a few of the boys smoking behind the gym. Went and told Delaney. Little snitch nearly got me expelled."

Elliott was a prefect in middle school and part of his role was to report back to Mr Delaney when students were doing the wrong thing. He took his role very seriously, and it's probably why he was school captain in Year 12. I could really see him forging a career in politics. The prefect and the rebel – natural born enemies.

"Well, you know he's my ex?"

I don't know why I say it. Maybe I want to hurt him just as the photo had hurt me, but I know it won't. He won't care that Elliott and I were once together. Elliott has nothing that Noah wants.

"You dated Harrowhill? Man, you have bad taste." He chuckles.

I give him a look.

"Present company excluded. Obviously." He winks at me but I'm in no mood for his charm.

"What are you doing here, Noah?"

"I'm getting a drink. Hey Willow! Can I get a coke please?" I'm unimpressed, and he can sense it. He turns to me, serious. "I came to see you. You didn't text me back, so I went to your house. Your mum said you were here—"

My ears prick up, and I interrupt him. "You saw Mum?"

"Yes," he says slowly like I'm a crazy person.

"How was she? Is she okay?"

"She's fine. Why? Shouldn't she be? I mean other than the thing – oh shit, does she know?"

I shake my head. "No. She was just—"

"Chelsea! How are those orders coming?" Pete yells out from the kitchen.

"Yep. Getting done," I shout back. "Look, I have to get back to work."

He grabs another handful of nuts. "So, I can't sit here while you do that?"

Willow plonks a coke down in front of him, and he winks at her. "Cheers."

"Don't you have friends to get back to?" I say flustered.

"Nah, they'll be fine."

"Well, you're distracting me!" I say, flustered and flushed.

"Then I'll sit here in complete silence, just watch you work like a creep, and make sure no one else bothers you."

I look at him. He is smiling at me completely unaware that I was mad at him just hours earlier. He is irresistibly charming, and I'm finding it difficult to stay mad.

"She'll get a break in an hour," Willow swings past and whispers loudly to Noah.

That mischievous grin returns, and I can't help but smile back.

True to his word, Noah sits in silence at the bar and watches me fulfil orders. It is less awkward than I thought it was going to be. Every now and then I look up and around the restaurant to his friends who don't seem to mind that he's absent from their group. The girl in the photograph doesn't look our way at all. Not once did Noah look at his phone to keep himself busy while standing watch over the bar. He simply watched and waited. I caught a glimpse of Elliott and his friends every so often, and they were a different story. I swear I could see the steam coming out of Elliott's ears. His eyes were fixated on Noah, locked on and ready to fire.

When it's finally time for my break, Noah follows me through the staffroom and out the back door of the restaurant to the same bench, under the same tree where Willow and I sat during our break earlier in the day. I feel like so much time has passed since then, and his solitary stance has softened my attitude. All that silence though gave me more time to think things through in my head, and I'm more confused than ever. He sits next to me on the bench, casually putting his arm around the back of my chair. I wriggle out of his arm and put a small amount of distance between us. He looks at me, confused by my actions.

"Alright, Roberts, spill." He removes his arm from the back of the chair and places both hands in his lap.

I'm not too sure how to approach it. We're not *technically* together (at least I don't think we are?) so therefore I don't *technically* have any right to be mad at him for partying with another girl. I also can't *technically* be mad at him for not texting me back straight away because friends aren't bound by the same rules as boyfriends when it comes to this kind of thing. Yet, I still feel betrayed and hurt. Instead of offering an explanation, I simply shrug my shoulders. I hate myself for doing it, but I can't find the words to say without humiliating myself.

He lets out a stifled laugh, rubs his beard and slouches back in the seat. There's an uncomfortable silence between us that hasn't been there before. He's the first to break. "We know each other's biggest secrets. I told you things that I've never told anyone, Chels. And now, now you're gonna pull this shit. Don't do it."

"Do what?" I raise my voice. Why am I making this harder than it needs to be?

"That same shit the rest of the chicks pull. If you've got a problem, say it. Talk it out. But don't make me try and guess. I fucking hate games."

"Games? You're one to talk about playing games."

I didn't mean it to come out as harsh as it did, and he is surprised. He looks hurt.

"Me? What games have I been playing, Roberts? Do enlighten me. Because I think I've been nothin' but good to you."

"Good to me? Sorry it was such a chore!"

He stands up in frustration. "Fuck Roberts! What's gotten into you? I thought you were different, but you're just like the rest of 'em. Playing mind games." He taps his head.

My eyes well up, and tears burn my eyes as they try to escape. This is not how I imagined the night or this conversation to go. I want to scream back at him, *so are you! You're not who I thought you were either. You're just like the rest of them too!* But I don't, I keep it to myself and watch him storm off back through the restaurant. I wait out the rest of my break under the tree alone, refusing to let the tears escape for fear they won't stop once they start.

I make my way back to the bar and begin to fill the last orders of the night. Willow has been placed on dish duty, so I'm alone at the bar. I look up once to scan the restaurant for Noah, but he has left, along with his friends. Elliott is still here, though, and his expression has softened. He takes my glance as an invitation to come over.

"Everything okay, Chels?"

I nod, barely holding it together. Everything is not fine. Not by a mile.

"Noah looked pretty pissed when he walked back in. You two have a fight?" He's being careful with his tone.

"There's no 'us two', Elliott. There never has been!"

"Okay! Okay! I just wanted to check that you were alright," and he looks genuinely concerned.

One look at those baby blues and those feelings of longing come flooding back. I want someone to hold me and take it all away – my dad, Noah – I want it all gone. Elliott is easy, familiar. I could feel safe again.

"Do you need a lift home, Chels?"

I shake my head. "Willow's taking me."

"I don't mind, honestly."

I know I should say no, but something inside of me wants Elliott to drive me home. I want things to feel like they did two months ago when Elliott was my boyfriend, and my dad wasn't having an affair and didn't have a secret family. I want to go back and erase the last two months and be who I was.

"Actually, that'd be great." I give him a half smile.

SIXTEEN

Willow tries to talk me out of catching a lift with Elliott. She and Elliott have a fight over me, but I stand my ground and ride with Elliott. Willow is unusually salty at me and tells me I'm making a big mistake before she storms off to her car, then speeds out of the parking lot. I don't understand what her problem is with Elliott giving me a ride home. Is she just worried I'll end up hurt again? It's too late for that.

Elliott opens the door for me and takes me home. He doesn't ask again about Noah. Instead, we fill the time with a trip down memory lane, reminiscing about the good times we had together.

"Hey, do you remember Jen Granger's eighteenth? It was Easter weekend, and we all had to dress up as something easter-y." Elliott asks with a sparkle in his eyes.

I nod. "Yes, you dressed up as a giant Easter egg with Ahmed and Cole." I laugh. "You guys even painted your faces to match your cardboard costumes."

"That stuff was hard to get off!" He's laughing at the memory now too.

"You had a purple face for days."

"I remember you dressed up as a pretty cute little bunny. It was actually kinda hot."

I look down and try to hide the smile creeping across my face. A bunch of us girls got together and dressed as matching bunnies. We'd ordered little blue and white checked dresses that fell to mid-thigh and wore white shirts underneath with cotton tails on our butts and rabbit ears on our heads. The pictures of the night are on the wall of my bedroom still.

"It was also the first night we said I love you." He looks at me and gives me a shy smile.

I smile back, not saying another word.

I remember.

When Elliott pulls up to my place, the house is dark except for a light on the porch. It's almost midnight by the time we make it home.

"I'll walk you to your door," Elliott offers, and I accept.

It's only as we stand facing one another under the light that we realise we are holding hands.

"Old habits die hard," Elliott says apologetically.

I smile at him. It certainly did feel like old times. Elliott has dropped me home many times after my shift at Pete's. We've kissed under this very porch light more times than I can remember. Many stolen hours were spent here, just the two of us as we struggled to say goodbye. I should thank him, say goodnight and walk inside, but I don't, I hold his gaze. He moves closer. With his free hand he cups my face and gently kisses my lips. I kiss him back, dropping his hand and snaking both of my arms around his neck, pulling him closer. This feels so easy, so familiar. Our bodies react automatically, like muscle memory. Elliott puts his hands around my waist, and I forget about Noah, my dad and the last two months spent apart.

"What the fuck?"

I push out of Elliott's arm quickly. I look guilty. He looks pleased. Noah looks angry.

Elliott stands in front of me as if to shield me. I push past him and walk towards Noah.

"Noah, it's not—"

He holds his hand up to silence me. He doesn't say anything, and we stare at each other silently communicating everything.

"You should probably go, Kalani," Elliott asserts.

I spin around and offer him a teary-eyed death stare.

"If anyone should be leaving, it's probably you, arse-munch," Noah growls.

He puffs his chest out and appears so much bigger. Elliott crosses his arms over his chest, stubbornly staying put under the safety of the porch light.

"We're in the middle of something, so if you don't mind…"

Noah lets out a low snicker and moves towards him. I place my hands on his chest, and he stops immediately, refusing to look at me.

"Noah," I whisper, urging him to look me in the eyes.

It takes a moment, but he finally does, and I see my own pain reflected in them. How could I let this happen? A moment of weakness ends in heartbreak. How could I be that easily distracted?

"Here," Noah holds out a black cylinder, "I did this for you, while you were away."

He backs away from me and doesn't say another word. I will my legs to chase after him, but they're stuck to the ground. I try to call him, but no sound escapes my mouth. Instead, I'm forced to stand and watch him drive away. A pair of hands cup my shoulders, and I violently shrug them off.

"Chels—"

"Don't!" I warn Elliott. "This was a mistake."

"Didn't feel like a mistake." He grabs at my waist, but I shake him off.

"I shouldn't have let you drive me home," I say to myself more than him.

Elliott paces. "I don't know what you want anymore, Chels. You keep sending me all these mixed signals—"

"Mixed signals? You offered to drive me home! Driving me home isn't an invitation to...to—"

"What about the kiss then?" he angrily interrupts me. "That's twice now you've led me on."

I shake my head. "No, I didn't mean to. I'm just really confused and—"

"Confused about what?"

"Everything! You, Noah," I leave out the part about my dad, but I imply it in the silence. "You keep popping up whenever Noah's around."

Elliott gently takes my hands in his and commands my attention. "I love you, Chels, and guys like Kalani just want to take advantage of girls like you. I want to protect you."

His lines seem rehearsed and ingenuine. The world feels like it's spinning. "I think you should go," I stammer, "I need to go and lie down."

Elliott sighs like he's annoyed that his little speech didn't work. He runs his hands through his hair and rubs his lips together. "Look, Chels. I love you, and I still want you to come to the party tomorrow. Just sleep on it. I'm sure everything will be clearer by morning." He reaches over and kisses me on the cheek.

I remain frozen to the spot and let him leave. This time I don't watch him go.

SEVENTEEN

Once I finally make it to my room, I rip off the lid to the cylinder and shake out its contents. As I unfurl the paper, I see me. Well, a drawing of me. Noah has sketched the photo of me in the sunflower field, only this time I'm looking at the viewer and my hair is shorter and pink. The tears that had threatened to fall pour out. The eyes he has drawn are so life-like. I touch them to make sure they're not. It's beautiful. I reach for my phone and see I have a missed message. It must have gone off in my bag before my shift ended.

N: Sorry about last night. I was a dick.

N: I'm just gonna come over and say it in person *winking kissing love heart emoji* #stalker

More tears stream down my face.

I frantically type a message to Noah, hoping I haven't ruined everything. I don't want Elliott. I want Noah, and now I may have lost him. I can't bear the thought. Noah is the one who makes me feel safe, beautiful – like I matter. I'm shaking as I type to him. How could I have been so stupid and messed up so badly?

C: Noah, I'm so sorry. Can we please talk? Can you please let me explain? I never, EVER, meant to hurt you. Please let me talk to you in person.

I cling to my phone like it is giving me life. Minutes go by without a reply. I try to call him, but the phone goes straight to voicemail. I try again. I send another message.

C: Your drawing is beautiful. I love it more than anything. Thank you. It made me cry. Please, Noah, please let me talk to you. *sunflower emoji*

Two hours go by, then three, then four and before I know it, the sun is about to rise. I've had no sleep. Elliott texted me when he arrived home, saying he was looking forward to seeing me at the party. I don't reply. I don't want to see him. I want to see Noah. I wish I knew where he lived, then I would have Mum drive me over there and beg him to listen to me.

I move through the next day on autopilot constantly refreshing my phone and checking all platforms for any sign of life from Noah. It's closer to dinner time when I make one last ditch effort to get Noah to hear me out. I call again. It goes to voicemail. This time, I leave a message.

"Noah, it's me. If you text me your address, I will come to *you*. Please Noah. I'm sorry I didn't speak up last night. I was scared because I didn't know where I stood with you, and I was scared to ask. I didn't want to be rejected because I like you so much. I was feeling hurt because I thought we had something special and when I went away you ignored me and brushed me off. Then Willow sent me a picture of you and some girl together and all the comments made it seem like you were a couple. I was hurt. I was confused. I know now I should have just said something. I'm so sorry. I'm having a hard time coping with all this stuff with Dad too. Elliott just caught me in a weak moment. Please let me talk to you in person. Noah, I'm so sorry and—"

The phone cuts me off. My frantic ramblings have been silenced.

There's a stain that runs from my eyes, down my cheeks and to my jawline. I fear it's permanent. I refresh my messenger every few seconds hoping a new message will appear. My phone buzzes, and I jump, fumbling my phone in my fingers.

E: Hey babe, where are you? Thought you were coming tonight?

It buzzes again.

W: Chels! I'm at Elliott's! Where are you?

I text them back the same brief message.

C: Sorry. Can't make it.

Willow doesn't reply. Elliott is quick to respond.

E: Are you with him? What happened after I left?

I begin to type a response, but Elliott is too quick. I can tell he is furious.

E: Whatever Chels. I'm done. Thought I was missing out on something lately but last night reminded me that I'm really not missing anything.

I scoff out loud in disgust and disbelief that he would send me a message like that. I curse myself for being so foolish and letting him back into my life. His message is like reopening an old wound, and Noah's silence is the salt.

I cry.

I sob.

I can't stop.

I never knew my heart could hurt like this. I want the pain to stop. It's too much. It's all too much; Noah, Dad, Elliott – I can't deal with all of this anymore. I can hear some altruistic voice in my head chastising me for my choices and causing so much pain. I see flashes of Dad and his mistress at the hospital and then again at the zoo with their family, and it's all too much to take. I want the noise and the pain to stop. I walk over to my desk and scan it for a sharp object.

I see the scissors.

My heart races.

I pant.

I pick them up and stare at them in my hand.

They're heavy.

Cold.

I scream.

I throw them across the room. I want to replace this feeling inside me with something else, some outside pain, but I can't. I can't do it. I feel like a failure. I want to run away. Run away from myself, escape my own skin, but I feel trapped. I can't break free.

I climb into my bed and hug my knees to my chest, heaving as I try to control my breathing. How did it all come to this?

EIGHTEEN

I can't sleep.
I have no more tears left to cry.
I can't move.
Everything is broken.
I am broken.

NINETEEN

I relive every moment since the hospital as punishment. Mum delivers food throughout the day and calls Pete to tell him I won't be in for my shift. I text Willow and tell her the same thing. Dad pops his head in at one point, and I pretend to be asleep. He doesn't disturb me and shuts the door behind him as he leaves. When I'm awake, I shift between staring at my phone and the ceiling. I've run out of tears. The day blends into night. The smell of dinner snakes its way upstairs and makes my stomach turn. I haven't been hungry all day.

TWENTY

I hear her voice before I see her standing at the foot of my bed. I don't make any effort to get out of bed, instead I sit up to greet her.

"You look like shit, but you don't look sick." Willow says, swaying shopping bags in my face. "Chocolate chip biscuits, snakes, Tim Tams, black forest chocolate block, these new weird marshmallow chocolate biscuit things and there's a tub of Ben and Jerry's in the freezer downstairs. I've already told your brothers that I'll murder them if they touch it."

Willow pounces on the bed and empties the contents of the shopping bags. There's at least two of everything she listed.

"How did you know?"

"Please. I saw those sappy quotes you've been posting online. Ha! Elliott thinks they're about him but I'm like, yeah right. Why would you be posting about him? Clearly this is all about Noah. After the picture I sent you, and you calling in to work sick, I just kinda put it all together."

"Mum told you, huh?"

"Totally. To be fair, I put it all together after she told me." She leans over and gives me a hug. "I had no idea you two were that serious!"

It has been three days since Noah showed up on my doorstep and gave me the drawing, the one hanging in pride of place above my bed. I open up the Tim Tams and take a small bite. I still don't feel like eating, but they're my one true food weakness.

"Yeah, well none of it matters now, not after the whole thing with Elliott." The thought makes me want to hurl.

"Elliott?"

I look at her, confused. "You said Mum told you…"

"She said you and Noah had a big fight. Was he super pissed because Elliott dropped you home the other night?"

"We kissed. He saw us." I duck my head.

"Chelsea!" she sounds annoyed. "I told you getting him to drop you home was a bad idea. What were you thinking?"

"I wasn't, okay? Things have just been stressful lately and then this whole thing with Noah – it was a huge mistake. And now…now Noah won't even talk to me. I don't blame him either. I thought Elliott would have told everyone at the party."

Willow shoves one of those marshmallow things in her mouth. "No, the prick left that part out."

I twirl the edge of the doona around my finger. I start to speak, but Willow cuts me off. "Look, Chels, I'm sorry I haven't been around much this summer. I've been a bad friend.

Things have just been, I don't know, different since we finished school, you know?"

I nod. They have been different, but she hasn't been a bad friend. If anything, I have. I'm the one keeping secrets from her. She shouldn't be apologising, I should be.

"Willow—"

She holds up her hand. "Chels," she interrupts, "I feel like there's so much to talk about and—"

My phone buzzes and silences us. I stare at it for a moment wondering if I'm strong enough to withstand a message that isn't from Noah. A message from anyone else will feel like further rejection from him. I check the time. 9:15pm. I swipe at my phone.

"It's Noah," I say to Willow.

"What does it say?"

A simple text with an address. A tsunami of relief washes over me. I spring out of bed and throw on whatever I find on the floor.

"It's his address. Will, can you drop me there?" I say urgently.

"Now?" she sounds disappointed.

I nod. "It has to be now. Please, Will."

We arrive at a small brick house that looks like every other brick house in the street. There are a few garden gnomes scattered about the front lawn as Willow and I walk up the path to the front door. I convince Willow that it is okay to leave me and that I can make my own way home. I feel a little uncomfortable with her around anyway. There is still so much she doesn't know, and I can't risk it slipping out now. One problem at a time.

"Are you sure? I feel like I'm betraying the sisterhood if I just leave you here," Willow says dramatically.

"I'll be fine, Will. Besides, he invited me over. He's not the type of guy who's just going to leave me abandoned in the street." I hope.

She hesitates before agreeing with me. "Okay, fine! These gnomes are giving me the creeps anyway. Look, text me and let me know you're home safe later, okay?"

"Sure. And thanks again, Will, I owe you one."

"Just remember you said that." She hugs me and fast walks back to her car.

As I approach the front door and knock, I'm hyper aware that I'm probably waking his elderly grandparents and that it's past an acceptable hour for visitors. I run my palms over my shorts to wipe away the sweat gathering in my hands. As I wait for the door to be answered, I begin to regret not taking the time to make myself more presentable. This is going to be the first time I meet Noah's grandparents, and I want to make a good first impression – well, at least good enough that they will forgive me for coming over so late. Instead, here I am bare-faced, dressed in cut-off shorts and a tank top. Even my hair is a mess, thrown back into a tangled bun.

An elderly gentleman answers the door, and I feel my body racing. I'm nervous that he'll yell at me, and I really don't want to upset Noah's grandparents. I want them to like me. Maybe it's too late for that now. Would he know who I am? Would he know what I've done? I hurt his grandson; he has every right to slam the door in my face.

"Hi, I'm Chelsea. I'm a friend of Noah's. I was wondering if he was home?" I twirl the bottom of my top in my hands.

The man looks unimpressed although he is still dressed in a shirt and dress pants which means I didn't wake him from sleep. A small win. He looks like an older and shorter version of Noah. And one with less hair. I definitely see Noah's eyes and hope they're kind like his too. Right now, they don't seem to be.

"He's out back. Go 'round the side gate. Should be unlocked if he's expecting you." He shuts the door in my face. I guess Noah gets his directness from his grandfather.

I use the torch on my phone to find my way to the side gate and reach for the handle. There is a hole in the gate to unclasp the latch. I reach through and hear a rustle in the bushes just behind the fence, followed by a low growl. I immediately retract my hand. His grandfather didn't warn me about a dog. This is not a good sign. He already hates me. So much for a good first impression.

"Banner. Come here boy," a whisper and a whistle. My stomach dances at the sound of his voice. "Roberts?"

"Yeah, it's me," I say nervously. Partly because of the dog, partly because of him and what is about to happen. Good or bad.

The whole ride over, I kept thinking about what I wanted to say, but my brain wouldn't cooperate. Every time I thought about what to say, I was distracted by Willow's driving. Was she going the right way? Was she sticking to the speed limit? Couldn't she hurry up? It's only now, standing at his gate, that I realise I have no idea what I'm going to say to Noah.

"Come on, boy, she's okay. She's friendly. Good dog."

I wait for the gate to open. There is no way I'm attempting to open it a second time. The dog quietens down, and the gate creaks open. I wince at the thought of more noise and making Noah's grandfather even crankier.

"It's okay, he won't bite. But you'll have to come say hello, so he knows you're friendly."

I gulp. I love dogs. We've always had them but this one, even in the dark, looks big and definitely sounds scary. My dogs have always been more afraid of their own shadows than anything else.

"It's okay," he says to the dog, and to me, "just put your hand in front of him. Let him sniff you."

I do as Noah instructs and much to my relief, the dog licks my hand. I pat him around the ears, and Noah praises his dog. I let out a large breath. I follow the two of them around the side path and into the backyard where a bungalow sits nestled in the garden. I imagine it's a really pretty sight in the light of day. The night lights only give a mere glimpse of its true beauty.

The bungalow is a small circular shape. A large double bed fills the middle of the room, and a couch and recliner sit in a semi-circle corner that is set up like a lounge room, fit with TV, stereo and stacks of vinyl records. On the other side is a large drawing desk with a lamp and tins full of different drawing tools. It looks like the most lived-in spot in the whole bungalow. Noah sits on the couch, and his dog curls up next to him, letting me know exactly where I stand. I'm delegated to the recliner.

"Noah, I'm so sor—"

"You said that." He interjects.

I'm taken aback by his abrupt manner. This is a mistake. It's over. I can see that now. Being here is my punishment. I search for the right words but can't seem to find them.

"I'm not gonna make you keep apologisin'. You said you were sorry. I accept."

I look at him confused. I hate confrontation, but I need to explain, maybe so it makes sense in my head, or maybe so he understands just how sorry I am. I need to apologise, but he stops me before I can say another word.

"Show me the picture."

"I'm sorry?"

"The picture Willow sent you. The one that made you lose your shit."

I grab my phone and show him the message. He looks at it for a brief moment before tossing the phone on the couch. He moves towards me, bent down on his knees, and places his hands on my thighs. Goosebumps spring up along my legs. Banner stays put but keeps a watchful eye over us, ready to pounce at any given moment. I am a little uncomfortable.

"You don't ever have to question my loyalty to you. That picture," he points to the phone, "is a picture of me and Stace. We've been friends since kinder. Nothin's ever happened. Nothin' ever will. That's just how we are. We muck around."

"But the comments—"

Noah rolls his eyes. "People post crap. Come on Roberts, you're smarter than that."

I believe him. When I look into Noah's eyes, it's like looking directly into his soul; I know he's giving me the truth. In fact, that's Noah: honest and direct. It's not in him to lie. Between everything happening with my Dad and Elliott, I jumped to conclusions and made a fool out of myself.

"You'd probably like her," he gives me a wry smile, "she told me to stop acting like a baby and give you a chance to explain."

I do like her. I make a mental note not to judge anyone ever again.

"When I saw you and…Harrowhill…" I wince, and he doesn't finish his sentence. "Anyway, I sulked for a bit. Stace kicked my arse and told me to talk to you. I believe her exact words were "grow the fuck up and go talk to her"."

We share a small laugh.

"Why didn't you message me back when I was away?" I hate myself for asking. There is literally no way to ask that without sounding like a needy, stage five clinger, but I need to know.

"I was workin' on a deadline. I've kinda been slackin' off since I met you." He gently squeezes my legs. "I had to get some work finished otherwise I would have lost the contract." I sink into the chair feeling sheepish. "And I was drawing your picture. I kinda get lost when I draw."

We have that in common. I should have known. I'm such an idiot. "I'm sorry." I whisper. It is all I can manage.

"Just ask me next time, yeah?" he leans in and kisses me.

I don't deserve it - the kiss, his forgiveness – but I let go of everything I have been thinking and lose myself in the moment.

"Wait, wait," I stop mid-kiss and push him back, "Elliott."

"I don't want to know." He shakes his head.

"But I feel really awful about it, like, I cheated on you." I duck my head.

He kisses me again. "Forget it. We weren't technically official so…"

"So…?" I need more confirmation. I need him to say it. I need to hear it. Good or bad, just say it.

"Well, now we are. If that's what you want?"

I grab him with both hands and kiss him. "Yes! That's what I want."

"But," he says in between kisses, "if I see Harrowhill again, I'm gonna punch that motherfucker out."

Noah lifts me into his arms, and I curl my feet around his waist. He walks over to the bed, lays me down and gently kisses along my collarbone. I run my hands through his hair. He lifts up my top, exposing my bra and lightly kisses a trail from my belly button to the nape of my neck. My body is shaking, a mix of delight and nerves. I'm not ready. Not now, not with everything else going on. I place my hands on Noah's shoulders and gently push him back.

"Stop. Stop," I say to Noah gently and pull my top down. "I don't think I'm ready."

Noah sighs and runs his fingers through his hair. "Okay. We'll wait."

He doesn't seem annoyed or disappointed.

"Really?" I ask.

"Yeah," he kisses me again, "I'm not gonna force you to do somethin' you're not ready for."

"Even though I've done this before with someone else?"

"Cheers for bringing that up, Roberts." He mocks. I apologise. "Seriously, ready whenever you are."

"What if it, like, takes a while? To be ready?" I shrink into myself, afraid of his answer. Noah is older and probably more experienced than me. He isn't going to wait forever. He looks at me, seeming conflicted about whether or not to say what he is thinking. I close my eyes, bracing for impact. "My mind is all over the place, and I don't want to ruin anything with us. I want it to be perfect and—"

He puts his fingers to my lips to quieten me. They're soft. Warm. "I mean it, Chels. I'll wait for as long as it takes." He looks at me again with those same worried eyes, conflicted about how to proceed. It makes me uneasy. "Stuff it," he removes his t-shirt, "you were gonna see it anyway."

Even though I've seen him shirtless before around the pool, I still find myself getting giddy over his carved body. He turns to the side and lifts his arm. I see the scripture, the quote inspired by his grandfather's words, and then I spot it. A new piece of ink that wasn't there before. A sunflower, no bigger than a fifty-cent coin. My hands are drawn to it. He tenses when I touch it.

"Cold hands," he flashes me a nervous smile.

I am speechless.

"I got it while you were away, Chels. I'm not showing this to you to make you sleep with me or feel bad for not sleeping with me." He hesitates over how to approach what he wants to say next. For the first time, Noah is uncertain. It's a little unsettling to see him so unsure. Noah has always been so confident. "And I hope it doesn't scare you off. I got it for you or to remind me of you."

I sit with my mouth hanging open. This is hands down, the craziest, most surreal, most romantic thing anyone has ever done for me. I don't know what to do with myself.

"I've never felt this way about anyone before, Chels."

"What if it doesn't work out?" I whisper, afraid of the answer, afraid to even think about the end before it's even begun. But that's what I do.

"Then I'll have a reminder of how great we were. Or I'll just get it lasered off." His joke breaks the tension in the small bungalow. "You know, I like sunflowers. They're strong. They turn their backs to darkness and follow the light. Example to live by, I reckon."

I think about what he says. I've never thought deeply about flowers before; they're pretty and smell nice, but around Noah, I find myself thinking about all sorts of things I've never thought about before. Sunflowers find the light and shine despite the shadows around them. It's a great metaphor for life; there will always be darkness but there will also be light: choose which to follow. I like my sunflower dress even more now. Maybe I should get a sunflower tattoo too. That'd really freak my parents out. Noah keeps his shirt off, and I cuddle into his arms as he settles back onto the bed.

"Think I'm a ragin' psycho now?"

I shake my head. "No. I think it's really sweet."

I'm a little embarrassed by how much he cares. Not because I don't want it, but because no one has ever cared for me like this before, and I don't know how to show him how much I care for him in return.

"There's something else I have to tell you, Chels." Neither one of us move from our embrace despite the seriousness of his tone. "I'm goin' to Europe at the end of the month. It's a one-way ticket."

I look up at him: one-way ticket?

"I had this all planned before we met," he continues. "I want to go over and see all that art and history for myself. Be inspired by something." He shrugs. "I just need to go. I can't really explain it. I just don't connect with being here. Not you," he kisses me to make a point, "I definitely connect with you. Call it a spiritual awakening or whatever, I just need to…fly, you know?"

I smile and think back to what Nanna said about her trip, and how it helped her grow and connect to herself in ways she never could have, if she had stayed here. I don't want to hold

Noah back, but I'm terrified of what this means for us. We've literally only just become an us. What does that mean, now?

"But you have a one-way ticket." I say, disappointed.

"I wasn't sure when I was comin' back."

"Or *if?*" I look at him.

Noah nods and strokes his beard. "You can't just go on a coupla nature hikes and swim in the ocean for a coupla weeks and be like "hey man, I found myself. Here's a picture of me and some famous old building." People that do that and post it all over social media are shallow dickheads."

I trace the outlines of his tribal tattoo on his chest, avoiding the elephant in the room. His skin breaks out in small goosebumps.

"Come with me."

"What?" I sit up.

"Come with me. I mean, what have you got here? A course you don't want to do, and a family that's messed up."

"I can't just leave, Noah."

"Why not?"

I can't think of a solid reason why I can't go with him, not one that he wouldn't have an argument back for anyway. I have some money saved up that could get me over there, and I suppose I could always work to support myself. It's true, I really don't want to do my uni course. And my family – oh, my family! What would happen to them? How would Mum or my brothers cope with the secrets and betrayal without me? They need me. We need each other to get through the storm that is brewing. I have to stay. I *want* to stay. I can't leave my family in the midst of a crisis.

"It's not that easy for me, Noah. I have so much going on here—"

"Exactly! Time away would give you some perspective."

"What about uni?"

"Fuck uni. You don't even want to be a journalist. Defer it." His defence is quick.

"What about money?" I know I'm in the middle of a losing battle here.

"I have some. We'll support each other. Get jobs." He has it all figured out.

"What about *my* family? Mum? The twins?"

"Your brothers probably won't give a shit you're gone, and your mum's old enough to handle herself. What are you really afraid of, Chels?"

"I don't know! I haven't had time to think this all through! This isn't part of the plan." Panic rises in my voice.

He chuckles and brings my hand to his mouth to kiss it. "That's your biggest problem, Roberts, you overthink things. Just let go. Do something spontaneous!"

"And you're too spontaneous!" I smile.

"We're a perfect match then."

I eye his new tattoo. "I need some time to think."

He smiles at me. "Alright."

"Alright," I say back.

I curl back into his arms, and we lie on the bed thinking about the future.

TWENTY-ONE

I don't stay the night in Noah's bungalow; he drops me home just before midnight with the promise we will see each other the next day after my shift. When I arrive home, I pass Mum and Dad curled up on the couch together, asleep in front of the TV. They look so content, like a regular happy couple. Only I can see the lies that sit between them. It has me thinking though: what if I keep Dad's secret? I could go away with Noah to Europe and not have to worry about anything back home. Like he said, I could gain some perspective about the whole situation. But what if Mum found out while I was gone? It would break her. Who would she have to support her?

I find it difficult to go to sleep; I toss and turn thinking over Noah's proposal and all the possible outcomes. I know tons of people who take a gap year after finishing school. I could name at least ten from my year alone! Could I do it, though? It was never part of my plan; my parents had made their feelings on gap years well known for some time.

If you take a year off, you'll never go back to it, was my Dad's argument. *We've paid good money for your education, too good for you to just throw it all away on an Arts degree*, was another hit stuck on repeat of the Dad Lecture Series. They make me feel like I owe them something for my education, like I have to finish university in a parent-approved course before they will be satisfied with any adult decision I make in the future.

Mum is less outspoken when it comes to my future. Actually, I don't recall her saying much at all, just agreeing with Dad. She went to university, studied sports medicine and then put her whole career on hold to be a full-time, stay-at-home mum. Dad kept her comfortable enough that she didn't need to return to work, and I don't think he really wanted her to either. With her at home taking care of the kids and the house, he was able to focus on his career, which I find hypocritical of him. He pushes me but never pushed her. I wonder what Miss Glossy Hair does and if he pushed her to return to work after popping out his illegitimate children. The thought angers me and makes me even more restless.

I get up. I turn my desk lamp on and in the low light of the night, I write a list of pros and cons about Europe.

PRO
1. Time alone with Noah
2. Adventure
3. No plans, free to roam as we please
4. No uni
5. Hello! It's EUROPE!!

CON
1. Time away from my family when they need me
    most
2. Money – how can I afford this? Terrible exchange
    rate
3. No plans! Where will we stay? Eat? Work? Can we
    work?
4. No uni – how long will this put off my career?
    (What career? Is that a pro?)
5. I don't speak any language other than English

TWENTY-TWO

As I walk into work the next morning, Pete greets me with a frown. He's probably still upset with me for getting Mum to call in sick instead of doing it myself.

"Well thank God you showed up! Willow rang me ten minutes ago to say she wasn't coming in!" he snaps. "It's going to be impossible to find someone to replace her at such short notice!"

I didn't know she was sick. Normally, she'd message me if she wasn't going to be in. Pete tells me I have to work a couple of extra hours, we all do, to cover the hours and work Willow is missing. I sigh. Noah is picking me up after work, and I'd rather spend those extra hours with him. I feel guilty for being annoyed with Willow when she's sick.

I walk through to the staff lockers and pull my phone out of my bag to message Noah about staying back. There is a message on my phone, but it's not from him or Willow. It's from Jen Granger. I haven't heard much from her since exams finished, which is strange, now I think about it, because I always thought we were good friends. I have heard people say that you lose touch with your friends once you leave high school. While I feel a bit sad that I didn't really notice Jen's absence, I really hope Willow and I don't drift any further apart than we already have. I open the message and am surprised with what I see. It is a picture of Willow and Elliott. Kissing. I send her a quick message.

C: What is this?

I hear Pete call out my name, but I wait by my locker for a reply.

J: I'm sorry C. Just thought u should know

C: When was this?

J: Elliotts party da otha nite xo

I don't know what to do with this information. I stare at the photo a little longer before I begin to recognise those same emotions that I felt when I saw Dad and Miss Glossy Hair.

Disbelief.

Anger.

Confusion.

Numbness.

How could either one of them do this to me? I immediately forward the picture to Willow and Noah. I don't know why him. I guess I just want someone else to be as outraged as I am. Pete calls out for me again, but Noah and Willow message simultaneously.

N: I'm confused, Roberts. Is this your attempt at foreplay? Who are these people? *crazy face emoji*

W: Chels, I can explain. It's not what is seems. Meet me after work xxx

I don't bother texting either one of them back. Pete calls for me, and I know this is my last warning before he loses his cool. I head out to the restaurant and begin to serve customers.

The place is not busy enough to take my mind off the photo Jen sent me. I can't believe Willow would do that to me. Once upon a time, I didn't think Elliott would either but lately, nothing surprises me regarding him. As I serve pancake stacks to happy families, I wonder how long the two of them have been seeing each other behind my back. Right now, I'm angry more than anything else. The more I think about it, the more dots I can connect; the way Willow has been bringing Elliott into conversations all summer, her distance and her moods. Were they together when we were? Is that the reason Elliott suddenly dumped me? No, she wouldn't, would she? She's my *best* friend!

Noah arrives just before the end of my shift. He winks at me as he makes his way over to the bar and takes a seat, picking at the nuts in the bowl on the bar top. I walk past him with empty plates on my way to the kitchen. He places his hand on my hip.

"You alright, Roberts?"

"You got my text." I snap as if that is the only explanation he needs.

He screws his face up in confusion. "Yeah. Bit weird. But if that's what you're into—"

"It's Willow and Elliott. Kissing. At a party."

He shrugs it off and takes a sip of his drink. When he realises that I'm waiting for a response, he quickly swallows. "Sorry, am I supposed to say something here?"

I roll my eyes and storm off. I avoid walking past him for the rest of my shift. How could he not see what a betrayal this is to me? My best friend and my ex. She has broken the girl code. And lied to me!

When it's time to clock off, I walk out without collecting Noah first. I hear him run after me calling out my name. "Whoa! Hold up." He turns me around and leans me against his car.

I fold my arms across my chest. He places his hand over the top of my head, stopping me from opening the car door. "Don't be mad at me; I'm not kissing Willow!" He uses his free hand to jerk my chin in his direction, so I look him in the eyes. He pulls a silly face, and it makes me laugh.

"Stop it, this is serious," I say a little less serious than before.

He shrugs. "Don't worry about it, Roberts, you're with me." He leans in and kisses me deeply. I unfold my arms, roll my shoulders back and my lips fall in step with his.

"But she's my best friend, and he's my ex. You just don't do that," I protest when we stop for air.

"Who gives a shit?"

"I do! I care. What if this has been going on behind my back all along? This is just like Dad." My chest begins to rise and fall rapidly.

Noah grabs me by the shoulders and gets me to follow a slower breathing pattern, like he's my coach. I calm down with his help.

"Cut the drama, Roberts. Just go talk to her." He gives me a knowing look, a reminder of the last time I let myself jump to conclusions and the problems it caused. "Then you can freak out once you know the full story. Until then…" he kisses me slowly and never finishes his sentence.

I send a message to Willow agreeing to meet. Noah drives me to her house, and she's there waiting for us in the driveway. I feel bad having to deal with this on our time together; it just seems like there's always something going on. I'm not use to this much drama. Normally my life is uneventful. I managed to avoid all the high school drama. When girls were fighting with each other over boys at a party, you'd find me in the kitchen eating snacks, or while girls were in the bathroom at school crying over some fight with their bestie, I was in the art room, drawing. Now, my life is more drama filled than an episode of "Gossip Girl", and I'm not here for it. I just want things to go back to the way they were.

Seeing Willow in the driveway makes me worry about what she's going to say. She's dressed down in her sweats and her hair is thrown into a messy bun: very unlike Willow. She's always so well put together, even first thing in the morning she looks like a magical pixie. Right now, she looks like a pissed off pixie whose magic dust has been stolen.

I tried to prepare myself for all possible outcomes on the drive over while Noah kept telling me to be calm and go with whatever happens. *You can't change it*, he had said to me, *you can only deal with it*. I take a deep breath as I walk up the driveway to greet my best friend. My ex-best friend? I'm not quite sure where we stand right now. Noah follows behind me. To Willow's credit, she doesn't ask him to leave.

"I'm so glad you came," she says, her anger melting slightly as she gives me a hug. I don't put my arms around her. Why is she so angry? She's in the wrong here. "Chels, this is not what it looks like."

My eyes adjust to the dark, and I can see, even from the single light on the porch, that she has been crying. Noah stands behind me with his hands in his pockets. The warmth from his body makes me safe; like I have some sort of protective shield around me that would deflect whatever she was about to say.

"Chels, he kissed *me*. I mean, I was a little drunk and kissed him back, but he set it up. He made sure Jen had her camera ready and took the picture. I swear, like a second after that photo was taken, I pushed him away." She is talking a million miles an hour.

"What do you mean, set you up?"

"I heard him ask Jen if she got the picture, and then they walked off together. I don't know what happened after that."

"So, she just took the photo and walked off?" I don't quite believe her. Why would Jen do something like that?

Willow nods furiously. "Yes! I guess the plan was to send it to you and make it seem like we've been sneaking around."

Noah snorts. Willow gives him her best evil eye. "It's true. It's posted online too. That's where I've been all day, at Elliott's house yelling at him and getting him to remove it."

I rub my temples. Everything is spinning. "But you said you kissed him back. Why are you so angry?"

She shifts on the spot and throws her head back, letting out a groan. Noah takes a small step closer to me to steady me for what is about to come. He senses something in her stance.

"Okay, look. We've been talking this summer."

"Talking?" my voice rises.

"Well… you've been busy with *him* all summer," she motions towards Noah, "I've been kinda lonely. And it doesn't matter anyway because he keeps coming back to you."

"Is that why you're so angry?"

She lets out a sigh of frustration. "God, Chelsea! You have no idea how annoying it is to see you with *him*," she points to Noah, "and then listen to *Elliott* talk about you or go running back to you every time he gets jealous."

She takes a step closer, and Noah pulls me closer to him and away from her.

"It's harmless flirting, Chels."

"That turned into a kiss."

I can't believe she is trying to blame this on me because *I* had been *busy* with *Noah*. Really? I want to shout at her and tell her everything. I want to tell her about my Dad and whilst she thinks I've ditched her for a guy, I've really been trying to deal with the biggest secret I've ever had to keep. Her kissing Elliott is not my fault.

"Chels. Look, I liked him in high school too." *You liked everyone in high school*, I want to shout, but I don't. "He asked me earlier in the summer if I wanted to hook up casually, but I said no, Chels."

I scoff. "Yeah, well, he asked me the same thing on New Year's, and I turned him down too." She stares angrily at the ground, kicking a stone. I feel my face flush as I remember that I haven't told Noah about that yet. I give him a hesitant look, and he strokes his beard.

"I'm really confused by all this. Basically, he wanted to hook up with both of you over the summer, and you both said no. *You*," Noah points to me, "don't show up to his party. His little ego is bruised so he tricks *you*," pointing to Willow, "into kissing him, so *he* can get someone to take a picture and send it to *you*," points to me again, "so you two will *fight* and he'll feel like King Dick."

Willow and I shrug. "Basically," we say in unison.

"Righto." Noah spins me around and kisses me before spinning me back to face Willow. He gives me a gentle nudge forward. "You two have some shit to work out. I'm out. Call me tomorrow."

Before I can stop him, Noah walks to his car throwing the peace sign at us behind his head. Willow and I stand stunned in her driveway. Once Noah drives off, Willow and I avoid each other's gaze. Instead, we both focus on a spot on the ground in front of us. I can't believe any of this is happening at all.

"Um…should we go inside?" Willow stumbles over her words, unsure how I will react.

I nod and follow her. Her place feels like home to me. Her parents are already asleep, so we quietly make our way through their perfectly decorated house and into Willow's bedroom. Willow's room is a lot like mine; double bed, desk and clothes all over the floor. The complete opposite to the rest of their immaculate show home. This room though, feels like Willow. Her personality is all over it. There are fairy lights running along the roof of her room and above her bed are a series of pictures placed in the shape of a love heart. There are at least two dozen photos up there and I feature in most of them. My shoulders hunch over at the memories on the wall and the position we're in now.

My phone buzzes with a message.

N: Tell her about your Dad.

I shoot him off a quick reply.

C: Thanks for ditching me. And you better not be texting and driving.

N: Relax mum, stopped 4 petrol. Just tell her. Shes ur best friend.

I know Noah's right; I should tell her. She is my best friend, and I haven't kept a secret from her in all the time we've known each other. People knew that telling one of us a secret meant telling both of us. She said she was feeling lonely without me. Maybe if she understood where I've actually been these holidays then things will get back to normal. This whole mess with Elliott is his doing, not hers. Despite my anger, I can see that. When I look around the room, I'm reminded of our friendship and what that means to me. I send Noah back a series of kisses and promise to call him tomorrow. I am actually going to take his advice.

"Will, there's something I need to tell you," I say sheepishly.

She sits on the bed and pats a spot right beside her for me to sit. I take up her offer.

"Before I do though, I just need to know something."
She lets out a sigh, bracing for my question, "did you and Elliott
ever hook up while we were together?"

She shakes her head. "No. I swear to you on the life of
Zac Efron that we only kissed once at his party. The rest has
been stupid flirty messages," she looks down at her fingernails,
peeling away the chipped black paint.

I let out a long sigh, letting go of all the anger and hurt.
Noah is right, I'm with him now, so none of it matters. I choose
our friendship. I choose forgiveness.

"So, what is it that you want to tell me? You're not
pregnant, are you?" She gives me a small grin and I return the
gesture.

I tell her everything. I tell her about the hospital and the
zoo. I tell her about visiting my grandparents and the fight with
Noah. Although she knows parts of that story, she stays silent
and listens. I tell her about Elliott, and she shifts uncomfortably
on the bed. I tell her about Noah catching us together, and I feel
sick reliving the memory. I tell her about Europe; but most of all
I tell her that I don't know what to do – with any of it.

She nods her head and thinks. I look down and twirl her
blankets in my hands.

"Why did you wait so long to tell me all of this? Idiot!"
She wraps me into a hug, and I let out a few tears I didn't know
I was holding on to.

"I don't know what to do, Will."

"Well, I think this proves that: one, Elliott is an A-grade
arse hat," I nod in agreement, "and two, Noah is the knight in
shining armour, and you should totally marry him and have his
babies."

We laugh. It feels good to have my best friend here with me. I feel like I'm finally coming up for air. I ask her what I should do about my Dad. "Noah thinks I should confront him and make him tell Mum."

Willow shakes her head. "I don't think you should."

Her response surprises me. I honestly thought she would agree with Noah. I was hoping she would help give me clarity, but now I fear I'm more confused than ever.

"If you do that, Chels, you might back him into a corner. What if he just leaves? What if he chooses his other family over yours? I mean, this whole situation is not ideal, but I think you need to stay out of it."

"But it's my family! Don't you think Mum has a right to know."

She nods. "Yeah, I do. But what do you know? Do you know for sure he's their father? I mean, little kids say things all the time that aren't true. How do you know the kid just didn't get confused because he's been around a bit?"

She's right, I don't know for sure. I just know that Dad didn't correct the kid when he called him Daddy.

"Did you see him with the kid?"

I hesitate. "No, I just heard them—"

"Well, how do you know it was them then?"

"I know my dad's voice, Will."

"Okay. Then what? You confront him. Give him an ultimatum. Fine. But what if he doesn't choose you?"

I haven't really thought about that. I just assumed he would choose us; we're his real family. They came along second. It's not fair for him to choose them. Mum is his wife.

"I think you should try talking to him about what you saw or *think* you saw, but I don't think you should rush in guns-a-blazin.'"

Yeah, none of this is any clearer.

TWENTY-THREE

The next day, Willow and I troll Elliott on social media. We send him a picture of the two of us looking happy and laughing from last night with the caption, "Nice try, dickhead". We tag him in photos of the two of us, and Willow even tags him in a meme that says, "Chicks before dicks". He gives us complete radio silence, so we know we've made him mad.

Noah comes over sometime in the afternoon, and we spend the day not doing a lot more than kissing and talking about nothing much in particular. He stays for dinner, and it makes for an awkward night. Dad is home, and Mum insists on us all eating together like a family. I try and make a last-minute run for it with Noah, but Mum pleads with me, saying it would be nice for Dad to "finally meet your boyfriend." I reluctantly agree even if it is just because I like the word boyfriend when she refers to Noah.

Noah and I share looks at the dinner table as Dad lays on the PDA with Mum. He's especially attentive tonight. Is he trying to show off in front of Noah, or is he fearful someone is onto him? Dad refills Mum's wine glass and places his arm around the back of her chair, rubbing her back occasionally. They smile and steal looks at each other through dinner like lovesick teenagers. Noah and I are acting more like adults than they are.

"So, Noah, tell us a bit more about this freelance job you have," Dad asks.

I take in a sharp breath. I know Noah will be polite, but I can't say the same for my father when expressing his views about a career in the arts.

"Well, people employ me to design things for their company. Graphic design."

"Did you go to university to study for this…*career*?" he adds, the last part like it's a joke that no one is in on. I know what he's trying to do. He's trying to expose Noah's lack of academic credentials. After all, that's what matters to him.

To his credit, Noah doesn't miss a beat. "A short course here or there, but I haven't needed to. The work speaks for itself."

Dad forces a smile. "So, the work is steady then?"

I give Dad a stern look which he ignores. Noah leans into the table to pour himself another drink and shoots off a grin, "Haven't had a problem yet."

I place my hand on Noah's knee under the table as a show of support. Dad nods, sipping at his wine. "Yes, I assume you must be very talented. Noah, tell me something, how *do* people find you. You're not attached to a company, or a *real* one…"

I squeeze Noah's knee as a warning not to take the bait. He places his hand on top of mine. Message received.

"That's right. I work for myself. I have a website and social media. My folio's there; you should check it out sometime. I think you'll be surprised at some of the *big* companies I've done work for. But it's mainly word of mouth."

"Do you ever go looking for work," Dad lets out a little chuckle to disguise his passive aggressive attack, "you can't just expect work to land in your lap."

Noah sucks in a deep breath, and I can tell he's working hard to keep it together. "Yep. I put submissions in. Get them too. But I'm finding I have plenty of work, so I don't really need to go looking."

They eye each other. Mum breaks the tension, adding her two cents. "The job landscape has changed dramatically over the last ten years," she says, "I read something the other day that said that the jobs our boys will be going into haven't even been invented yet. Astonishing! How can they teach and prepare you at school for the workforce if they don't even know what they're preparing you for? It's madness."

"Yes darling," Dad chimes in, "but there will always be a need for people in traditional careers like medicine and law. Anyone can get a job, but a career…," he shakes his finger, "it seems everyone these days has their own side business."

"Side business," Noah mutters under his breath, and I get the double meaning.

"Sorry, Noah?" Dad inquires.

"Have you ever had a *side* business, Andy?" Noah fires back, and I squeeze his knee again, harder to let him know I noticed the "Andy" dig.

Dad shakes his head, oblivious to what Noah is really asking. "My job keeps me pretty busy."

"I bet," Noah replies. "Yeah, I don't do *side* businesses either. This is my business. I'm very loyal to my business and will stick it out even when things get hard. When things turn to shit, I'll stick by my business."

There's confusion on everyone's face although the twins stifle a giggle when Noah swears. Mum shoots them a warning look. I understand what he's saying, what he's really talking about. Part of me is swooning over his public declaration for me and for us, even if it is hidden. And part of me is so mad at him for treading so close to revealing the biggest secret I hold.

I clear my throat. "Noah's very passionate."

"Well, it's great to see someone so young and so passionate about what he does. Good on you, Noah." Mum smiles and raises her glass to salute him.

"Hmm," Dad rubs his chin, "yes, there is a lot to be said for the younger generation. But good on you for giving it a go, Noah." He too raises his glass to join Mum in a toast.

Noah begrudgingly raises his water and plays the game.

After dinner, Noah and I watch a movie together in the lounge room. My brothers join us and leave a trail of popcorn around the room. When it's time for Noah to leave, I walk him to his car.

"Man, I need a drink! Your old man is a piece of work," Noah states angrily as we stand by his car.

"I know. I'm sorry. You did great though." I kiss him.

"Have you thought more about Europe?" I pull away shaking my head. I don't mention the list. Noah continues, "You don't want to stay here for *that* do you?" He points to the house, indicating Dad.

"I just need to figure out what's going on here first. He's still my dad."

"Yeah, and the sooner you tell him and put him back in his place, the better."

I jerk backwards. "Noah, he's still my dad. His secret affects my whole family. This will have a huge ripple effect on everyone."

"I know. The smug prick has it coming. What did Willow say?"

"She thinks I shouldn't say anything. She thinks I need to find out more."

Noah shakes his head and paces. "This is ridiculous, Chels! She's wrong. You know you need to confront him. The longer you hold onto this, the worse it's going to get for everyone."

"I think we should just say goodnight before you—"

Noah stops pacing and looks at me. "Seriously? I'm just being honest. The guy's a dick. He cheats on his wife, on his *family*, tries to trap you into a future that you don't want, thinks *I'm* a joke, and you're still standing up for him?"

"I'm standing up for my family."

"You're stalling."

"Excuse me?" I snap.

"You're stalling. Just get on with it."

"For someone who doesn't like drama, you sure are in favour of creating a lot of it." My head is spinning. I wonder how this escalated so quickly.

"Me?" he lets out a laugh of disbelief. "I'm in favour of the truth! I know what keeping secrets does to people. To families. My whole family was ripped apart by my mother keeping her secret for so long." He flings his arms around and makes gestures as he speaks. The angrier he becomes, the wilder his gestures are.

"And this could tear mine apart, and I don't want that!" I yell back.

"So, you're happy living a lie, are you? Having this secret eating you up inside, making you feel like shit while he gets away with it."

"I didn't say that—"

"I just…" he sighs. He takes a deep breath to calm himself and grabs me around the waist to pull me closer. His voice softens, "I just want you to be free. To be happy." He kisses me and I resist, refusing to move my mouth with his. He pulls away. "Chels."

"Can't you see how big this is?" I say softly.

"I know more than anyone how big this is."

"Then why can't you support me?"

He pulls me in close again, and I allow him too. I relax my shoulders and rest my hands on his chest. "I do, Chels. One hundred percent." I let him kiss me and this time my mouth mirrors his.

"I'm scared about what will happen. I'm scared of breaking up my family," I whisper.

He lifts my chin. "Hey," he speaks softly, "it's not you breaking up your family. He did. Besides, you don't know how your mum will take it."

"As if she'd stay!"

Noah shrugs his shoulders. "Ya never know."

I wrap my arms around him and stay in his arms in the driveway for a while before he eventually leaves. I wave goodbye and go back inside.

I can't stop thinking about what he said. I never even entertained the possibility that Mum might choose to stay. That she might choose forgiveness. To me, this is a deal breaker, clean cut. I can't imagine staying with someone who not only cheated on me but on the family we had built together. But that's the point isn't it? This isn't about me. This isn't about my relationship. But if Mum chooses to stay, what does that mean for us? My brothers and me? Our family? I'm not sure I can forgive him for betraying our family. Where does that leave me?

Maybe I should go to Europe with Noah and figure all this out from afar, that way I won't be sucked in and forced to play a role in the drama. If I'm gone, it will be one less thing for them to worry about. Urgh! I'm going around in circles. I'm never going to get anywhere with the what if's. I need to do something. Noah's right. And I need to do it now.

TWENTY-FOUR

I find Dad in his study. He is reading over some important looking documents when I knock on his door. I've never had to knock before but just walking in feels too casual for what's about to go down. He looks up at me with a half-smile on his face; it's in the low light of his desk lamp that I realise how tired and worn he looks. He leans back in his chair and tells me to come in.

"You don't need to knock." He lets out a soft chuckle.

I shrug. "You seemed busy." I wipe my hands on my skirt as I walk over to the chair opposite him. I feel like we're in an interview, and it's making me even more nervous.

"Noah seems like a nice kid." I nod with him. "Seems pretty devoted to his little business. Hope it works out for him."

A smile stretches across my face. "I think it will."

There's a silence that neither one of us knows how to fill. It hasn't always been this awkward with him. I know what I need to say, but I don't know where to start. How do you tell someone you know about their secret family? Especially when that someone is *your* dad. They didn't cover this in the How-To-Be-A-Brilliant-Daughter manual. My stomach is churning, and my hands start to shake. I try to steady them. Deep breath. This is it.

"Dad."

"Yes, Princess." His eyes are focused on the documents in front of him.

"Dad, I need to talk to you about something."

He puts his pen down and leans forward to show that I have his full attention. He turns his head to the side and slightly narrows his eyes at me, as if I'm a patient and he's deciding on a diagnosis.

"Do you need to talk to me as Dad or Dr Roberts?"

I shoot back a similar look, then it hits me, and I feel my cheeks flush. "No. No, no, no, no. Not that. Not anything like that."

He lets out a sigh of relief. "Good. It's just…well, it hasn't gone unnoticed around here how," he is searching for the words, "affectionate you and Noah are. And he is a bit older than you…"

I shake my head and wave my hands in the air; please make this conversation stop. "Nope. Nothing to worry about, Dad. Promise."

Oh God, this is not how I pictured this going. I'm losing my nerve quickly. The thought of discussing my sex life – my non-existent sex life – with my father is too much.

"Well, you know you can always come to me—"

"Yep. I know. Thanks. Not what I wanted to talk to you about. At all," I interrupt. Can anyone see a black hole that I can dive into?

"Okay, okay," he concedes, "I may do this for a living, but it doesn't make it any easier for me to bring it up with my own daughter." He relaxes into his chair, and it tilts backwards ever so slightly. "So then, what did you want to talk about?"

I swallow hard.

I can't do this.

I.

Can.

NOT do this.

"Um…well, Noah has asked me to go to Europe with him, and I'm thinking about going."

Coward.

I didn't feel confident, and I let one little thing side-track me and throw me off. I roll my palms into fists and release them slowly. Nothing inside of me is slowing down though. I've missed my opportunity. Lost my nerve. Now I'm discussing something with him that I'm not sure I even want. Dad stays quiet, nodding to himself, thinking it over.

"What about uni?" he finally asks.

"I can defer."

"And how will you pay for it?"

"I have a bit of money saved up in my car fund." I actually have no idea how I'm going to pay for it or where we're going to stay. Or even which countries we're going to or how we're going to get around. Europe is a big place. Wait, is my passport even valid? I actually know very little about the trip as a whole and the thought sends me into a mild panic.

"How long for?"

I swallow hard at this question. He is definitely not going to like the answer. I quicken the speed at which I roll and unroll my hands. I don't know whether his short, sharp questioning is going to lead to a blessing or a lecture.

"A couple of months," I lie.

He goes back to his silent, nodding stance. I feel compelled to add more. "I can get a working visa and wait tables." I pause. "Or bar work. Pete's given me a bit of experience in that. I'm sure he'll write a reference." When he doesn't look impressed, I add, "Or I can do something else?"

"Such as?"

Inside, I am kicking myself. I shouldn't have said anything. I am about to lose this battle, and the more we speak, the more I want to win. But do I want to win to be with Noah or to beat Dad at something? "I'm not sure. We'll figure it out."

Dad lets out a small chuckle. "Figure it out? This is Noah's idea, right? Because the Chelsea *I* know likes and needs a plan. The Chelsea *I* know likes to know exactly what she is doing and when. This kind of spontaneity isn't your shade, Chelsea. And what happens to your studies? Where will this lead you?"

"I don't know!" I snap, fighting back tears.

"That's right. There will be plenty of time to travel once you have your degree. I just don't see why you need to go right now. I know it seems important while you're in the blossoming stages of a new romance, but, Chelsea, come on. You've known the guy for five minutes, and now you want to take off halfway around the world with him? Just drop everything you've worked hard for…for some *boy*."

I want to say that we've known each other for years, but the truth is, we only ever knew *of* each other. We never really spoke until a few weeks ago, but in that time, I've gotten to know him better than people I've known my whole life. I want to explain to him how deep in my soul I know that Noah is special and that this is more than just a holiday. This is a chance for me to learn about myself, figure out who I am and what I want in life. I want to tell him what Nanna told me, to make him understand, but I can't find the words. I want to tell him that I need to get away from him, my father, because ever since I discovered his secret, I've felt like the walls of the world are closing in on me, and I'm feeling trapped. I need to break out.

But I say nothing.

I keep quiet and sit there with my head down because after all, I'm nothing if not compliant. I hate myself for it.

"If he likes you that much, he'll wait for you and if he doesn't, well then…"

I nod and stand. "If that's it then, I think I'll go to bed."

"Night, love."

As I turn away, tears fall down my cheeks. Tears of sadness for Noah, for Europe and for myself. Frustration engulfs me, and more tears stream out. Why didn't I just go through with it? How could I let myself be pushed around again? I need to stand up to him. I need to stand up for myself. I slam my bedroom door shut and slump behind it, sobbing into my hands. I just want to be free.

TWENTY-FIVE

Work keeps me busy over the next couple of days, and I'm relieved to have a distraction. At least at the parlour I don't have time to think about anything other than pancakes and shakes. Willow and I are on the same shifts again and back to normal, while Noah is busy finishing a contract. I haven't had much of a chance to see him, and our communication has been strictly text only. I try to respect the fact that he has work to finish, so I keep my texts minimal, and he tries his best not to ignore them again like last time.

When we finally have the day off, Noah picks me up early from my house to get the most out of the day together, and I almost pounce on him as soon as I hop in the car. It's true what they say about absence making the heart grow fonder; although it's only been a couple of days, I've missed him and couldn't wait to have him all to myself. I'm also almost certain he grew hotter in the last couple of days. He is wearing his usual uniform of boardies, a tank and piercings along one ear. His beard is trimmed although to the untrained eye it looks no different, and he's taken to wearing his hair up in a bun more often after I told him I liked that look best on him. Yep, definitely hotter. I've styled myself with a messy bun too and am wearing my sunflower dress for him. The way he looks at me in that dress makes me feel like the most beautiful girl in the world. I like that feeling.

Noah drives us down the peninsula to wine country to pick our own strawberries. After confessing my love for the fruit, he said it was sacrilegious that I had never picked my own before. He promised they tasted better when you picked them yourself, and Willow agreed with him. She had been standing behind me at the bar at Pete's Pancake Parlour when Noah brought up the idea. We invited her along because it seemed rude not too, and I'm more aware now of making sure she doesn't feel left out after we talked things through the other night. She declined, and I won't say it was what I was hoping for, but I'm so glad to have Noah to myself for the day.

Noah is an expert strawberry picker. We've been sent to the green flag area along with everybody else and I'm sceptical about there being any strawberries left to pick.

"The trick is to go to the other end of the field where there's no one. You see, everyone sticks to the top of the field and fills their punnets, leaving the back end full of juicy strawberries." He leans down and removes a strawberry from its stem. "You also have to look *in* the greenery, not just around it."

After we've picked our own punnet – and I can now attest that strawberries do taste better when you pick them yourself – we sit in the café and talk over a sample platter of strawberry-themed desserts. Heaven.

"This place is amazing." I stuff another succulent chocolate-coated strawberry in my mouth.

"You know, those things are an aphrodisiac," he grins, pointing to the plate.

"Everything is an aphrodisiac to you."

He raises one eyebrow, leans in and kisses me. "Not like I need the help."

"Easy tiger. My dad already thinks we're going at it like wild rabbits." Noah throws his head back and laughs. "It's true! I went to talk to him about everything the other night, and he thought I'd come to him confessing I was joining Teen Mums." This makes Noah laugh even harder. "He said it hadn't gone unnoticed how "affectionate" we were with each other."

"Hey look, if he's handing out free condoms, I'll take them. That shit adds up. I mean, the way we're going through them and all."

I playfully give him a little shove. "Ha. Ha. Very funny."

"So, how did it go anyway?"

"The sex talk?"

Still chuckling to himself, Noah asks, "No, the other thing! What did he say?"

I shake my head. "I chickened out. He threw me off with all that other stuff. But I did tell him about Europe."

Noah looks unenthused. "Let me guess, he rejected it." I nod, and Noah throws his hands up as if to say of course. "Not surprised. Whatta ya think?"

I don't really want to get into another argument, so I shrug my shoulders and kiss him playfully, biting his lip; a strategic move to avoid confrontation. It fails.

"Ah-uh, not getting out of it that easy, Roberts. Spill. Europe. Thoughts."

I pout, but he's not having any of that either. "Fine. I still don't know. There's just so much that you don't even know about the trip. Like, where will you stay, how will you afford it, when will—"

"*We*. Where we're stayin'," he interrupts.

"Whatever. The point is, I need a plan. I need to know what I'm doing and when, but there is no plan. And when there's no plan, I freak out." I don't mean to sound like my father, and I'm not sure I even agree with his assessment of me. Perhaps I'm only like that because he is, and I've never had the chance to find out what I'm like because I've always followed his plan. I didn't know I was thinking all of that until right now.

Noah chews on a strawberry as if he's thinking over the right thing to say. "I see that." He grabs my hand and places it on his ribcage where the sunflower tattoo sits under his tank top. "I'm yours, Chels. I'm not gonna keep talkin' about it coz, shit, I feel like I keep gettin' rejected. And I'm not gonna beg. Just know, you won't have to worry about a thing. I got you. And…I want you to come. But if you don't, then that's cool. I'll respect that, but I'm still yours. Here or there."

I nod and smile because it's all I can do. No words form. I'm speechless; again. How does he keep having that effect on me? He leans in and kisses me softly, slowly, making it feel like time is standing still. I want to live in this moment forever.

Noah and I spend the day exploring the beaches nearby. Although it's summer, in true Melbourne fashion, the weather has suddenly turned. The clouds threaten to burst open at any moment. There's nobody in the water, and only a few people here and there, walking along the sand like us. We smile as we pass them, making the obligatory comment about the inconsistent summer weather. Noah makes me laugh, over what, I don't remember, but being with him is so easy. I feel the most myself when I am with him. Conversation is easy; even the silence is easy. I find myself more and more drawn to him each time we're together. I've never felt like this about anyone before.

True love.

I thought I was in love with Elliott, but now I realise I wasn't. I never had that sense of belonging when I was with Elliott, like we were two pieces of a puzzle that click together. Noah is my other puzzle piece; I am sure of it. When we're together everything just clicks into place, and a sense of calm washes over my soul.

A loud crack of thunder brings me back from my thoughts and makes me jump into Noah's arms. Forked lightening appears shortly after over the bay. Whilst a summer thunderstorm is stunning, the open beach is not a place you want to be.

"We'd better get back to the car," I announce.

Noah takes my hand, and we run along the hard sand with water crashing at our feet, taking with it our footsteps. The rain pours down on us and by the time we reach Noah's lonesome car in the car park, we're soaked through. The rain is so heavy that we cannot see out of the windows. Thunder roars on top of us and lighting cracks in front of us over the water. The clouds are grey and moody. It is a spectacular sight, even if it's a little frightening.

"I shouldn't drive in this. Too dangerous." I nod in agreement. He's right. The rain is too thick. "We'll be right in the Jeep. Climb into the back, there should be some towels back there."

I climb over the middle console first, followed by Noah. We search for a towel or blanket to help dry ourselves off but all we find is drawing pads, pencils and a pair of runners.

"Shit! Sorry, thought I had one back here." He begins to wipe himself down with his bare hands, and I do the same. He takes his hair out and shakes it like a dog before flipping it back. I let out a little squeal as water flies from his hair at me, and he flashes me a mischievous grin. My dress is stuck to my body like a second skin, my face has water dripping down it, and all I appear to be doing is moving the water over my body instead of drying myself. Noah and I laugh at each other. He takes his shirt off and wrings it out on the floor of his car.

"Try this," he says, handing me his shirt to wipe my face.

It doesn't help. Bare chest and dripping wet, Noah is completely irresistible. Something comes over me, and I know this is going to be it, the moment I'm going to give myself to him. I'm ready.

I climb into his lap and snake my arms around his neck, running my fingers through his wet hair. He places his hands on my thighs and lifts the hem of my dress up with his thumbs. We hold each other's gaze for a moment before I make the first move, kissing him slowly on the mouth. He runs his hands further up my thighs to my hips and pulls me closer, letting out a low groan. Our lips part, and I pull my head back slightly. I drag my hands over his shoulders and down his chest before moving them behind me to unzip my dress. I attempt to peel it off, but I get stuck. We share a laugh.

"Need a hand, Roberts?"

"This was far sexier in my head."

Noah reaches up and helps me take it off. The dress makes a thud on the floor of the Jeep.

"You sure?"

I nod. "Yes."

Noah smiles. "If you want to stop at any time, just tell me, and we'll stop."

"I don't want to stop," I whisper.

I kiss him slowly and move into him, our hips touching over our underwear. I definitely don't want to stop.

On the way home, Noah stops by his house to change. I opt to wait for him in the car, so I can call Mum and ask if Noah can stay the night. It has been the best day of my life, and I'm not willing to let it end.

"Hi love," Mum answers, "did you kids get caught in the storm?"

"Yeah, we did. We waited it out. Noah wouldn't drive in it. Said it was too dangerous."

"Good. Very sensible." I can hear the smile on her face.

I get straight to the point. Noah wasn't going to be long, and I want to surprise him with the good news. "Mum, can Noah please stay over tonight? In my room?" My request is met with silence on the other end. "Mum?"

"Yes, I'm here. I'm thinking."

"I've finished school. I'm nearly eighteen, and I think it's time that you let me have my boyfriend stay over, in my room." My heart dances as I say "boyfriend".

"Having your *boyfriend* over isn't the issue. It's the 'in your room' part I'm thinking over."

"Please Mum?" I beg. Noah has resurfaced in fresh clothes and is locking the side gate. "Otherwise I'll just stay at Noah's." It's a powerplay I've never used before. Mum and Dad, probably mainly Dad, had a rule that I was never to sleep at Elliott's house, but he was always welcome to stay at ours – in the spare room. Mum and I both know that Dad won't like me staying at Noah's house and although I've never been one to disobey them before, we both somehow know that I'm staying with Noah tonight, with or without her approval.

"Fine," she huffs down the phone, "and you're right, you're nearly eighteen, almost an adult," she concedes. "Look, Dad's not home tonight anyway so can you just make it look like he slept in the spare room, so your brothers don't know? And don't say anything, because you know they'll take any chance they can get to rat you out."

Noah hops back in the car, kissing me on the cheek. He gives me a quizzical look and I mouth the word "Mum" to him so he knows who I'm talking too. He nods and starts driving towards my house.

"What do you mean he's not home tonight?" I can't hide my annoyance.

"He's got a lady in labour so it's going to be a long night at the hospital. He's going to stay up there to be closer to work. He'll be back tomorrow, sometime."

"Whatever," I roll my eyes, "so it's a yes then?"

"Yes. Just…you know, be safe and—"

"Yep. Got it. Thanks, Mum. See you soon." I end the call before it becomes awkward and turn to Noah. "Guess what?"

"I hate this game."

"Spoil sport! Mum is letting you stay the night!"

"In your room?" he raises his eyebrow at me.

"In my room!"

Noah fist pumps the air. "Shit yeah. I love your mum."

With my bare feet up on the dash, I turn the radio up, finally enjoying my summer holidays.

TWENTY-SIX

The next morning, Noah and I make a point of meeting in the kitchen as Cody and Chris are eating their breakfast. We make it look like we've slept in separate rooms, but we needn't have bothered, the twins couldn't care less. They have their heads in an iPad playing some new game they downloaded. Noah and I move around the kitchen in a delicate dance, trying to avoid touching each other, stealing glances at each other under our lashes and flashing knowing smiles at one another. Last night confirmed my feelings for Noah; it's love.

I just know it.

"Oh, Chels love," Mum races into the kitchen, searching for something, "Dad just rang. He said not to worry, he'll be home in time for tonight."

I look at her confused. "What?"

"The photography thing," she slams a draw shut, "he said he'll be home in enough time to get ready and take you. Apparently, his patient had a really rough time, he almost lost her." She is too distracted to relay the news with any sensitivity.

"What happened?" Chris asks, a worried look on his face.

Mum, suddenly realising the twins are listening, tries her best to sooth them. "Nothing, sweetheart, it's fine. Daddy saved the woman and her baby. They're all fine." She pulls him close and kisses him. I feel torn. Normally, I'd feel a sense of pride – my father the hero – but right now I can't be sure this isn't some elaborate lie to spend more time with his other family. I'll forever be second guessing anything he says.

"He also said for you to be ready by five." She turns to me with a quick grin.

I'd forgotten all about the photography exhibition. I'm dreading it. The thought of having to spend the night with my father makes my breakfast rise.

"Alright, well," Mum turns and places her hands on her hips. "I can't find the bloody book."

"What book?" I ask.

"That stupid book in which I'm recording my diet and exercise. I'm meeting with my personal trainer at the gym and I need the book. Have any of you seen it?"

The twins deny knowledge of its whereabouts in unison.

"I'm sure there's an app you can get to record all of that," I add.

Mum scoffs. "I don't even use the book let alone some app. I was just going to fill it in on the way there."

Noah chuckles and shares a smile with Mum. I like how easy this all feels.

"I'm already late! I'll just have to go without it. I'll be about an hour, okay? Chels, you're in charge. Boys, behave. Back soon."

The twins barely look up, and Noah and I give a little wave as she scurries out of the kitchen.

Noah stays all day and watches me as I get ready for the exhibition. The closer it gets to five o'clock, the more my hands shake – I can't even hold the hair straightener properly.

"Does it look okay at the back?" I ask Noah.

"Perfect." He looks at me with concern in his eyes.

"My hair, Noah. Is it straight at the back?"

"Nobody is going to look at your hair when you're wearing that dress." He loops his arms around my waist and kisses my shoulder.

I've picked a simple dress for tonight; long, black with thin straps. My blonde hair is straight, and I'm wearing as little make up as possible. I don't want to go. Despite Noah's insistence that I look good, I feel gross.

"How am I going to get through tonight?" I moan.

Noah shrugs. "You'll be right. Hey, tonight could be a good opportunity to confront him about everything."

I wriggle out of his embrace and dramatically flop into the chair. "Sure, why not just ruin the night further."

"My mum said she always wished she'd told me sooner. Said the longer she kept it a secret, the harder it was to confess. The more hurt she knew she was causin'." Noah sits back down on the bed, an arm's length away.

"How did she feel afterwards?"

"Shithouse."

"Great." I moan and move to sit on his lap.

"Hey, you'd still be doin' the right thing. You're not in the wrong here. He is."

"Then why do I feel like I'm about to break up my family?"

"He did that the second he hooked up with that chick. Not you. None of this is your fault, Chels. Remember that."

I rest my head on his shoulder, and feel my eyes get droopy. They become too heavy and I give in to the weight of them. Noah cups my face, rubbing my cheek with this thumb.

"I love you, Chels."

I open my eyes, lift my head towards Noah and look deep into his beautiful brown eyes. Just as I'm about to say, "I love you too", there's a knock at my door.

"Chelsea, you ready honey?" Dad makes his way in slowly and completely intrudes on our moment.

I shoot daggers at him. Are there any other ways he could ruin my life right now? I begrudgingly stand and collect my bag with force, letting everyone know just how mad I am.

The car ride to the city is long and quiet. Dad gives up making small talk not long into the trip. I pull my phone out of my bag and flick around on social media even though it makes me mildly car sick. Noah has just said he loves me, and I said nothing. Nothing! Who does that? I couldn't just quickly throw it out there to him as I left the house; there's a special time and place for saying your first "I love you", and it's not while your dad looks on, tapping at his watch. I'm so mad at him I could scream. I can't even enjoy the fact that my boyfriend said he loves me. That's massive! How am I going to fix this? I don't want Noah to feel embarrassed for telling me he loves me, and I don't want him thinking that I don't feel the same way. I can't call him with Dad next to me, and I can't just text him. You don't tell someone you love them for the first time over text message. I need to say something, so I type a quick message and send it off.

C: I'm so sorry about before. I heard what you said. I don't want the first time I say it to you to be over text. *love heart emoji*

N: I can wait *love heart emoji*

C: Come over tomorrow?

N: Of course try an enjoy the night xo

C: Wish I was here with you xoxo

N: Same. You look beautiful tonight. Cant stop thinkin about you.

C: *love heart emoji* *kissing face emoji*

N: *sunflower emoji*

TWENTY-SEVEN

We arrive at the National Gallery of Victoria to a red carpet and photographers. It is more glamourous than I thought it would be. I've never been to an opening night of anything before. It's stunning. The coloured lights over the stone wall and water feature make it look magical. It's hard to stay grumpy when I'm surrounded by such glamour! As we make our way in, we're stopped by a photographer who tells us he's from the *Herald Sun*. He takes our picture and names for the social pages. He tells us to look out for our picture in the paper tomorrow and on their social media pages. I think it's a hollow promise given the amount of people here, but it excites me nonetheless. I've never been in the newspaper before. It'd be kinda cool.

There are loads of people standing in the foyer of the gallery, sipping champagne and eating impossibly small food off trays being passed around by immaculately dressed waiters. The high-vaulted, stained-glass ceiling is lit up to show off its beauty. Dad and I are standing on the outskirts of the crowd when a waiter comes over and offers us both a glass of pink champagne. Dad takes two, passing one to me as the waiter glides off without asking for my I.D.

"To you Chels. To uni and the future." Dad tilts his glass forward ever so slightly and I bring mine up to tap against it. We both take a sip.

So, this is Art Dad. Art Dad is relaxed. Art Dad lets me drink in public when I'm underage. Art Dad is my favourite Dad. I wonder how many sides to my dad there are: Art Dad, Husband Dad, Cheater Dad…it's hard to keep up. I take a larger sip of my drink.

"Easy, Chels, you don't want it going straight to your head."

I grimace. Another one of these and maybe I can loosen up enough to forget that I'm mad at him for a night.

The MC calls everyone to attention and makes a long speech about the exhibition. He reminds me of my old history teacher, Mr Randle, who would spend the best part of an hour-long lesson rambling on about something other than the actual point. I follow the lead of those around me and clap at the right times. I juggle my handbag, my now empty glass of champagne and a napkin with discarded toothpicks that were once stuffed into very garlicky meatballs. Lucky I'm not seeing Noah after this.

Once the speeches are out of the way, we're finally allowed into the exhibition, and as I walk through to the first room, I'm overwhelmed at the size of the imposing prints. I lose myself in the people and places hung on the walls. Every grain of every photograph is perfectly imperfect. They're stunning. Dad and I take our time walking around the exhibition, with each photograph I melt more into myself and abandon my anger towards my father. Just for one night. Just for now. This can be like old times.

"It's incredible. Look at the shadows. Stunning," Dad exclaims.

Room after room we're greeted by a history of humanity over time. Each photograph is someone's story. If my sunflower photo was hanging on these walls, what would it say? What would people think? We move to another room and find some of my favourite photographers' – Cartier-Bresson, Lange, Karsh – stunning black and white imagery.

I stop by "The Migrant Mother", the most famous Dorothea Lange portrait of a mother and her two children. I've seen it hundreds of times in books and on the internet, but they pale in comparison to the real thing. It's striking and haunting at the same time. She looks so desperate, so lost. The feeling of hopelessness is captured so brilliantly by Lange that seeing it unexpectedly causes a lump to form in my throat. An image of Mum flashes in my mind. They share the same eyes, and I imagine this is the look on her face as she contemplates life with an unfaithful husband. The two children hugging her could be my brothers. I blink the image away.

"It's something else seeing all these famous photographs, isn't it?" Dad is wide-eyed with excitement.

I can't look at him. I smile and move on to the next photograph. His phone rings, and I turn around. He looks at it, his brows pointed down in frustration.

"Ah, I've got to take this, Chels. Work call. Stay here, and I'll be right back." He smiles at me and answers the phone but doesn't say anything until he's out of earshot.

He's not on call tonight. Something in me stirs, and I follow him back out to the stained-glass foyer. He has his back to me, pacing. He's rubbing his head with his free hand. The conversation looks intense. I immediately think back to what Mum said about Dad saving the life of his patient. Perhaps something has gone wrong; perhaps she isn't as fine as Mum said. I move through the small crowd of people towards him.

"Look, just give him some Panadol, and I'm sure his temperature will come down." Dad sounds frustrated.

I stop and try to hide near a group of people talking.

"He'll be fine. Trust me. No, I can't."

My heart drops. This doesn't sound like a work call. I pull my phone out and give Mum a call, begging her not to pick up, hoping she's on another call with Dad.

"Hi love, how's the exhibition."

I choke back tears.

"I can't. I'm here with my daughter. I can't leave," I hear Dad say.

"It's good, Mum," I cough to cover my emotions, "sorry, I meant to call Noah."

"Oh thanks, Chels," Mum laughs on the other end, and I look up to the colourful roof to hold the tears back, "that makes me feel loved." I close my eyes. "Okay, well enjoy your night, honey. I won't wait up, so I'll see you both in the morning."

I say goodbye and take a deep breath. This is my opportunity to confront Dad. I've caught him. I open my eyes and look for him. He is standing still now, smiling as he continues to talk on the phone. I walk towards him, and he quickly ends the call.

"Sorry, Princess, work call." A single tear falls down my cheek. "Chelsea, what's wrong?"

My body feels unusually calm, and my mind slows right down. The only thing I can feel is my heart beating hard against my chest, making it difficult to breath.

"Was it her?"

Dad looks confused. "Who? My patient?"

I shake my head; more tears roll down my cheek. "I know, Dad."

I want him to say it. If I have to say it out loud, I might just break. I don't even know what to call her. I don't even know her name.

"Chels, I'm not following. You know what?"

The words tumble out all at once, and I can't stop them. "I know about the woman. I know about your other kids." A look of panic flashes in his eyes. "I saw you with them! I saw you kiss her!"

Dad closes the gap between us and lowers his voice. "Chelsea, listen to me. I don't know what you're talking about–
–"

"You're a liar!" I yell.

People turn to look at us. Dad grabs me by the arm.

"Chelsea, you're making a scene," he says in a low voice.

I shake off his grip. "I know. I know everything."

I stare him down. He grabs me by the arm again and pulls. He hurriedly walks us to the courtyard out the back with the view of the city landscape, lit up like a dream. The buildings tower over us as if enclosing us in this space, in this secret.

"What are you talking about?" he hisses at me.

There are a small handful of people outside smoking, but he has dragged us over to a quiet corner where it is just the two of us.

"I saw you. I came to visit you on Boxing Day, and I saw you kiss her at the hospital. I followed you to her house. I followed you at the zoo. I saw you with your other kids!"

Dad's face goes red. "You followed me?"

"That's not the important part of this conversation!" I yell.

He paces and rubs his hands over his bald head. "Chelsea, I don't know what you think you saw—"

"Don't lie to me!" I scream, tears streaking down my face.

He tries to quieten me, but I don't care. I don't care who sees, and I don't care if I'm making a scene. I can't stop.

"Does your mother know?" His hands are on his hips.

I shake my head. He paces further, rubbing his hands over his mouth. He swears to himself.

"You have to tell her," I demand.

He scoffs. "It's not that simple, Chelsea."

"Yes, it is. Make it that simple."

"Look, you don't understand. Marriage and adult…stuff. It's complex. You're just a teenager, you don't understand!" he raises his voice.

I take a deep breath. All in. "At least I know right from wrong. You have a whole other family!"

He lets out an angry groan. He doesn't know what to say. More importantly, he doesn't deny it.

"You have to tell Mum." I sniff and wipe my tears with the back of my hand, not caring about the effect it will have on my make-up.

"Chelsea," he warns.

I take a deep breath, not allowing him to throw me off my next move. Not this time. "You have until Sunday. If you don't tell her, then I will."

TWENTY-EIGHT

My nail bed is puffy and red. I'm sitting on the couch jiggling my leg up and down. Noah is slouched and relaxed; with his arms outstretched, resting atop the back of the couch. There's some movie playing on the television, but neither one of us is really watching it. We're waiting for Dad to come home from work. It's been twenty-four hours since I gave him the ultimatum, and he hasn't said anything. He rang Mum earlier and said he wouldn't be home for dinner. Mum, none the wiser, is curled up on the couch next to ours, captivated by the movie. She makes comments every now and then, which I respond to with "yeahs" to cover the fact that I'm not really watching it. Just before 9pm, Dad walks through the door. Noah and I share a glance at one another; mine is nervous, his is concern for me.

"Hi love, busy couple of days at the hospital." Mum's sympathetic. It makes me want to hurl.

"Yes," Dad says, "Chelsea. Noah." He acknowledges us, and we nod in his direction. We don't say anything to him, instead we watch him closely for his next move. Three days. Now two. I was generous to give him that long.

"You look exhausted!"

"I am." He looks like a man with the weight of the world on his shoulders. In some ways, he has: our world. "I think I might just go to bed. Goodnight."

He leaves the room, and Mum lowers her voice as she speaks to us. "Your poor father, he's been working so hard lately."

I want to cry.

"I think I might head off to bed too. Goodnight you two." Mum walks over and kisses me on the forehead.

"Do you think he'll say anything tonight?" I whisper to Noah once Mum is out of the room.

He shakes his head. "Nah, I reckon he'll try to talk you 'round."

"I'm not giving in. Not now."

"Then I reckon he'll leave it 'til Sunday." Noah says casually.

"You think so?" I bite my finger where the nail used to be, causing a sharp pain to jolt up my hand.

"Yeah, he'll do anything to get out of it."

I hope Noah is wrong. I'm not sure I am strong enough to withstand another confrontation. My plan was to tell my dad I knew his secret, deliver the ultimatum and have him confess all of his sins. I hadn't planned on negotiations. I didn't think there was anything to negotiate. I planned on him denying it, but that never happened. Should I expect him to try to negotiate?

It takes a long time to fall asleep and even then, it's not a deep sleep. Every little murmur Noah makes in his sleep wakes me. Having enough of tossing and turning, I head into the kitchen just as the sun is rising and find Dad sitting there, dressed and writing a note.

"You're telling her in a note!" I cross my arms over my chest, my outrage evident.

"Did Noah stay in your room last night?" he continues to write, not looking up at me as he speaks. "You know the rules, Chelsea."

Was he seriously going to lecture me about my sleeping arrangements?

"Rules are meant to be broken. I learnt that from you."

He slams his hand down on the bench and makes me jump. He takes a deep breath and regains his composure. "While you're living here under my roof, Chelsea, you'll follow my rules."

"This is Mum's house too, and she is fine with it."

He chooses not to respond. He finishes his note and finally looks at me.

"Your mother and I are going away for the weekend. Your grandparents are coming to stay and look after the three of you. I've told them Noah is not to stay the night and you are not to stay with him." I open my mouth to protest but he cuts me off, "You are not the only one to make demands around here. You can see each other during the day, but I forbid you to spend the night together. Do I make myself clear?"

"Forbid?"

"Do I make myself clear?" he says, a little louder this time. I nod. He passes me the piece of paper he has been writing on. "This is the name and number of the place where we are staying if you need us, plus, a shopping list and some money for groceries. Nanna can take you food shopping. They'll be here just after lunch. It would be good if you could tear yourself away from your boyfriend and spend some time with them."

He brushes past me on the way out of the kitchen, cold. He's my dad, but I no longer know the man he is.

Nanna and Grandpa arrive just after lunch like Dad said they would. The twins woke up in time to see Mum and Dad off and were full of questions, mainly, "It's not fair! Why can't we go to Sydney?"

Noah sticks around to meet my grandparents, and just as I expected, they both love him. Living with his own grandparents means that Noah is naturally at ease with mine. I haven't had a chance to tell Noah about what transpired between Dad and I in the kitchen this morning. I don't think he'll take to Dad "forbidding" us to see each other after dark too well.

My phone buzzes. I had all but forgotten I had it on me. It's Willow wanting to catch up later today. I say yes. I have so much I need to tell her. We agree to meet at the donut shop later in the afternoon. I head outside to sit by the pool while Noah splashes around with my brothers. I don't know what they're playing exactly, but it's noisy and wet; lots of water flying everywhere. Grandpa potters around in the garden, and Nanna sits on one of the lounge chairs at a safe distance from the splash zone. I curl up to her, falling into a special hug that only a nanna can give.

"Never too old for a big old cuddle with your Nanna."

"Never," I smile.

We watch the boys play, and I feel a sense of pride. Noah has slid right into our family like it is exactly where he belongs.

"Something on your mind, Miss Chelsea May?" I shake my head. "Don't lie to me. You're a terrible liar."

I laugh. "How did you know?"

"I can just tell. Spill it kiddo."

I'm hesitant, unsure if she knows the real reason she's here. I want to talk to her about Dad, but it is far too dangerous territory if she is still in the dark, so I tell her about Noah and Europe, and how I'm still trying to figure out whether I should stay or go. Nanna listens as I recite my pros and cons, making a few adjustments to make sure I don't give too much away about Mum and Dad. Nanna doesn't interrupt me once.

"I love you, Chelsea," she kisses my head and snuggles closer.

I scrunch my face up. "I love you too, Nanna, but…no words of advice?"

"I think that's part of the problem, love. You have too many people giving you advice. I said my piece back on the beach. Perhaps it's time you started to listen to yourself."

I sigh. Sounds like something Noah would say. "But I don't know what I should do."

"Chelsea love, if we did everything we *should,* life would be boring. Sometimes you just have to take a chance. A chance at adventure, love, friendship. Forgiveness…"

Something in her tone when she says "forgiveness" makes my stomach flip. I test the waters.

"Yeah well, some people should just stick to 'shoulds' and 'borings'." The contempt in my voice is evident. It's clear I'm no longer talking about me.

"The life choices laid out in front of you are yours to make. There's risk, yes, but there's no moral obligation in your choices. That's the difference."

My eyes widen. She has to know. The way she is talking is far too serious for my little trip. If she does know, then I wonder how long she has known for? I don't think I could handle it if she has been keeping this secret from us for all of these years. I need to know the truth. I take a chance.

"Nanna, do you know?"

"Yes." She replies simply. Her voice breaks. "We haven't known for long, but we know. Your father has wanted to come clean on so many occasions, but it's not that simple. He told me you knew. I'm sorry, sweetheart. It must have been awfully lonely to keep that to yourself."

"I have Noah." I pull away from her. "This is what I don't get – how can it not be that simple? You do the wrong thing, you own up to it. How did it get so out of hand? I mean the oldest kid looks like he's four. That's at least five years of doing the wrong thing, including the nine months of pregnancy!"

"There's a lot that goes on that you don't know about, love. Marriages and families are a complex—"

"Yeah, he said that too." I narrow my eyes at her.

Have they rehearsed their responses together? I'm over being treated like a child. I may not be experienced when it came to long-lasting relationships and marriage, but it still seems pretty simple to me – you don't cheat on your wife and create a new family with someone else. That seems like pretty standard common sense, and not too complex to me.

"I need to go meet Willow." I cut our conversation short. I can see she is going to take her son's side and talk me into forgiving him, and I don't want to. I stand up and walk towards Noah. He sees me coming and swims to the edge of the pool. He runs his fingers through his wet mane to move it off his face.

"I'm going to meet Willow at the donut shop. Can you please take me?"

"Sure thing." He lifts himself out of the water and onto the edge of the pool, each muscle in his arms flexing and showing off. I hand him a towel, and he dries off before slipping on a t-shirt and thongs. He is beautiful. I'm reminded of this fact multiple times a day and wonder how I get to be so lucky to hold his heart.

I find Willow waiting for me at a table by the front window. She has our regular order waiting as I arrive; two iced chocolates and two white chocolate and salted caramel donuts. It's one of those fancy donut shops that serve you drinks in mason jars and have an eclectic mix of donut flavours. It's also the spot we have been coming to ever since we started high school. It's the place where we've had most of our serious talks. Today is going to be our most important discussion yet.

"Has Elliott been texting you?" Willow inquires as we dig into our delicious treats.

I shake my head. "He's the furthest thing from my mind at the moment."

She shrugs. "Well, he's been texting me saying how sorry he is and that it wasn't supposed to go down like it did. He claims he *really* likes me and wants to give it a proper go." We roll our eyes in unison.

"Does he really think that'll work?" I shake my head. "Boys!"

Willow scratches her nose and bites off a large mouthful of donut. There is a look on her face that I haven't seen before. Disappointment? Confusion? I'm not sure what it is. And why would Elliott be texting and apologising to her and not me? Clearly the photo was a set up to try and hurt me because he was jealous over Noah. We both agreed at her house that he was not worth our time but here she is bringing it up and feeling…something. Did she want to meet here to get my approval? Does she want to date my ex? I can hear Noah's voice in the back of my head, nagging me to just ask her. Be straight forward and get straight to the point like he does. I take a deep breath and give it a try.

"Do you *want* to date him?" I try my best to act as a thoughtful and concerned friend, when really, I'm a little disgusted by the thought.

Willow's cheeks flush, and she's flustered. "What? No! After what he did? Are you serious?" But I don't believe her. What do they say about people who protest too much?

"Will, you can do so much better than him."

"Anyway, forget about him. What's news with you?"

I don't really think this conversation is finished, but I'm glad for an out because it's making me uncomfortable. I have to choose my words carefully when it comes to Willow and Elliott. I don't want to see her getting hurt like I did, and I don't want to come across as a jealous ex.

I tell Willow about confronting Dad instead, and their trip to Sydney for the weekend. I tell her about Nanna knowing and suggesting I forgive him, and how everyone keeps telling me the situation is "complex", and that I'm basically too young to understand any of it.

"That's a cop out," Willow states around a mouthful of donut.

"I know!"

"What do you think's going to happen when they get back?"

I shake my head and keep quiet. That is the part that is scaring me the most.

"Will, what's it like living in a split family?" I look down at my dress.

"It is what it is. I don't really know anything different. I mean, my dad isn't really my dad, but he is, if that makes sense. I mean, he's been raising me since I was two, and I don't know my real dad. My stepsisters make it difficult. They hate me and Mum. They blame us for taking him away from their mum. Which is totally not what happened!"

"What did happen?" I have never asked her that before now, and I feel like a terrible friend. I remember we were in Grade 4 when I found out Willow's dad wasn't her biological father. It floored me. I couldn't wrap my head around it, but she acted like it was no big deal. It was then that I learnt what a stepfamily is and was thankful that mine was not like that at all. It all sounded far too complicated. Now, my family is the definition of complicated. Willow and I never talked about the ins and out of her parent's marriage, I guess, because what nine-year-old knows that kind of stuff? We never really talked about it because Willow never acted like it was a big deal. Her parents were happy, and that's all that mattered.

"Dad left Rochelle because they fought all the time. He met my mum *after* he had separated from her, but my stepsisters don't see it like that. I guess there was a pretty short overlap between the two. Then they found out his new girlfriend had a baby and it hurt them even more, I guess. I don't call him Dad when they're around. Once when I was little, and I called out to him, they lost it and told me that he was *their* dad not *mine* and pushed me to the ground. Split the top of my head open." She pointed to the scar along her hair line. I knew that story, but I guess it was more poignant now.

"Do you think it'll be like that for us with his other kids?" I ask softly.

"I can't really see you pushing two little kids to the ground. Your brothers? Well maybe…" she teases, and it lightens the mood. "Do you even know if they're his? I mean, what if they're like me and just call him 'Dad' because they're too little to know any better?"

I think about this. He never said either way. When I think back to the zoo, to how tender he was with the little boy, and how he didn't correct him for calling him 'dad', I just know they're his.

"He didn't say they were. But he didn't say they weren't either."

"Look, Chels," she holds her hands out across the table and I take them. She rubs the back of my hands with her thumbs. "Whatever happens, they're innocent in all this. Just like you and your brothers. Try not to be mad with them, yeah?"

I smile, holding back my tears. When I think about my brother's and how they'll respond to all of this, I can't breathe. They're too young to have their world crumble right now. They'll be teenagers in a couple of years, and they'll need a father figure more than ever then. What's going to happen to them if he's not around? Mum couldn't handle them if they went off the rails. My mind takes me down a dangerous path of destruction where there is no good outcome for them. I have to protect them. I have to be there for them.

TWENTY-NINE

The weekend passes slowly. Although Noah and I are more than happy to defy my father's archaic orders, we stick to the rules out of respect for my grandparents. Noah stays at his house at night but spends the days with me. There has been no communication from our parents which adds to my anxiety. My brothers are still oblivious to the change that is afoot and relish time spent with Grandpa. He takes the boys and Noah fishing on his boat on their last morning together. Even though the open seas do not agree with me, I wish I had gone with them to take my mind off everything. Mum and Dad are due home in the late afternoon, and I feel every tick of the clock. Nanna has offered to take me shopping, but I can't face the lights and the noise. I have enough noise swirling in my head, worrying about what is going to happen when my parents return. I opt to clean instead.

Mum might keep a tidy house, but my brothers are lazy. With her away, they have taken full advantage of not being pestered to put their things away. I busy myself with household chores until I have cleaned the kitchen table three times and vacuumed the house twice. I'm about to start rearranging the pantry when all the boys arrive home, showing off their catch. Noah proudly holds up fish after fish, explaining who caught what and the name of each fish. The twins and Grandpa join in, poking fun at the other. I don't really follow what they're saying, and each fish looked the same to me, but it's nice to see them all getting along so well.

Grandpa tells the boys to wash up while he sorts the fish into piles for freezing and eating. Thankfully they gutted and cleaned them down at the pier. I definitely couldn't stomach that right now on top of everything else. Noah rounds me up and pulls me in for a hug. He smells of salt and fish.

"Eww! You need a shower." I laugh as I unsuccessfully try to push him away.

He holds me tighter and nuzzles into my neck. "I've forgotten where your shower is. Maybe you should show me," he says in a low voice, and a cheeky grin spreads across his face.

I point to my grandparents, who are sorting the fish. "I can't!" I match his tone.

"They won't know."

I push him off and he gives me a pleading look. I give him a smile as I shake my head. "I'll get you some towels."

"Noah, when you're done, you can help me. We'll cook them on the barbie," Grandpa calls out just as we leave the room.

"And you, Miss Chelsea, can help with the sides," Nanna says.

Noah and I agree before heading upstairs to the bathroom. I fetch him a towel from the linen closet which sits directly across from the bathroom. I stand in the doorway and hand him the towel as he begins to undress.

"Mum and Dad should be home soon." I say, throwing my hair up into a ponytail.

"You sure know how to kill a mood, Roberts."

"Well, I was never hopping in with you anyway." I playfully poke my tongue out at him, "I wonder how it went?"

"Worry about it when it happens." Noah turns to the taps and turns them on.

"But I am worried. I'm worried now."

He chuckles. "Oh, I know. But you can't control what happened or how your mum took it, so just roll with it when they get back."

I throw my head back and lean against the door frame. "You're so casual, and I'm freaking out!"

Dressed just in his briefs, Noah walks over, places his hands on my shoulder and rubs them. The firm, deep pressure of his hands actually works. Slightly. "You'll get used to it." He bends down and kisses my neck.

It is long passed the time when Mum and Dad were expected home. Nanna and Grandpa exchange concerned looks over dinner when they think no one is watching them. But I am. I am watching them. I'm watching everything; I'm hyper alert to everything going on around me. The longer Mum and Dad take to return home, the more hyper-aware I become.

I'm not sure what Grandpa and Noah did on that BBQ, but the fish is unlike anything we have ever eaten from there before. Dad may be a master surgeon and doctor, but he's a lousy BBQ chef. Grandpa is busy telling another fishing story when Dad walks through the door and silences us all with his presence.

Alone.

I look to Noah, then Nanna. My heart starts racing. Where is Mum? Was Dad's affair so shocking and sad that she left us? Surely, she wouldn't leave her children with a man she now despises.

"Where's Mum?" Cody asks with such childlike innocence that it reminds me of just how young the twins are. They're not ready for this. They couldn't possibly be ready for this. *I* wasn't ready for this, and I knew it was coming!

"She's staying in Sydney for a couple of extra days." Dad can't look at any of us. He finds a spot in the middle of the table and fixes his gaze there.

He looks even more dejected than before. His shoulders are hunched over, he hasn't shaved in days, and his eyes have dark rings around them. None of these are promising signs. What have I done? Why did I force this upon my family? I clear my throat and excuse myself from the table, running upstairs to my bedroom. I frantically search for my phone under the clothes that lie scattered across the room. I find it hiding under the folded washing on my bed and immediately text Mum.

C: When are you coming home? Please don't leave us. Mum, I'm sorry. Please Mum. I love you xx

I clutch the phone to my chest as though it is the sole thing keeping me alive right now. I curl up under my sheets, and let the tears flow freely down my cheeks. I don't notice that Noah has followed me until he lies down, wrapping his arms around me and kisses the back of my head. He doesn't fill the silence, and I'm thankful for that. I'm having enough trouble trying to grab onto a single thought as it is. Besides, nothing he can say right now can make any of this okay. My mum isn't home, and it's all my fault. I outed the family secret.

We'd been happy; ignorance is bliss, isn't that what they say? Then I opened my big mouth. Why did I have to go and destroy everything? Why didn't I just leave it all alone? It wasn't any of my business. Dad was right; it wasn't my relationship or my marriage. I didn't have to follow him at the hospital or that day at the zoo. I didn't have to find out more, but I did. I pushed and pushed until I knew and saw things I couldn't forget. I pursued this. What right did I have to get involved? Now, it can't be taken back. I have permanently broken our family. I should never have listened to Noah in the first place. He was the one who kept telling me to do something about it all along.

I push into Noah, pushing him away with my body, sitting upright with a look of disgust on my face. "This is your fault."

"What?" Noah sits up, confused. He reaches out to touch me, but I push him away, harder.

"You. You kept pushing me to say something. Just because your family is broken, doesn't mean that mine has to be!" I yell at him through my tears.

"What are you talking about?" He's trying to remain calm, but I can tell I hit a nerve. Good. "Your family has been torn apart by your mother's affair, and now mine is too. You just wanted me to be miserable like you!"

"You're being crazy, Chels."

"Am I? This is all your fault. If you didn't encourage me to say something, none of this would have happened! My family would still be together!"

"Your dad was fucking around long before I was on the scene." Noah's frustration gets the better of him, and he's yelling too.

"Everything has turned to shit since I met you. Everything! My Dad, Elliott and now my mum won't even come home! I wish I never ran into you at the hospital."

"You don't mean that," Noah says softly.

"Yes, I do! If I didn't stop to talk to you, I would never have seen Dad kissing that woman. None of this would be happening!"

Noah shakes his head in disbelief. I can see the hurt in his eyes and feel it in my heart. I want to stop myself, but I can't. It's like someone else has taken over, and I'm no longer in control of my own body.

"If that's how you really feel then—"

"It is," I snap.

Noah picks his things up off the floor and shoves them into his backpack. He opens my bedroom door, then turns to say something. He stops himself and leaves without saying another word. I fall onto my bed, collapsing into uncontrollable sobs.

THIRTY

By the next morning, Mum still hasn't replied to my text. My mouth is dry, and my head is pounding; it feels like it's stuck in a vice. I want to stay in bed all day. There's no point in getting up. A gentle knock on my door takes me out of my own head. I expect to see Nanna there, but to my surprise it's the twins. They look how I feel – rubbish.

"What's up?" My voice is croaky.

Cody and Chris look at each other and silently fight over who is going to speak. Surprisingly, Cody stays quiet and allows Chris to speak. "Are Mum and Dad breaking up?" His voice wobbles as he speaks.

Tears well in my eyes. I open my arms and motion for them to take refuge under them. They do. The three of us curling up together on my bed makes me let out a little involuntary laugh. "You know, Mum would take a picture of us if she saw this."

The boys let out little chuckles as they sniff and try to subtly wipe away their tears. I sat with them last night when Nanna explained what was going on. She didn't give them the full details but enough so they understand the gravity of the situation. Watching their faces crumple and tears spill from their eyes was the worst thing I've ever had to be a part of in my whole life. I never knew my heart could break into so many pieces all at once.

"We heard you and Noah fighting. Are you breaking up too?" Cody adds.

I look up to the ceiling to try to stop the tears from coming. Noah. My broken heart shatters into more pieces. I was so mean to him. In the light of day, I can see that none of this is his fault. I was hurting, and I took it all out on the one person who means the most to me. Now I think I may have lost him.

"I don't know. I said some pretty mean things."

"Can't you just say you're sorry?" Chris' question makes my lip wobble, and I don't think I can hold it together any longer.

"Sometimes," I struggle to talk, "sometimes it's not enough."

"You can try though," Cody quips.

I nod. I can, and I will try, but I'm not holding out much hope. I think I may have pushed things too far this time. How do you forgive someone when she told you she wished she never met you?

My brothers and I lie together for a while. We avoid talking about anything to do with Mum and Dad. Instead, we talk about random things until the boys are feeling brave enough to face the day. After they leave, I pick up my phone: no messages. No missed calls. No notifications of any kind. At that moment, I don't know who I want to hear from more – Mum or Noah? I lie in my bed a little longer, absent-mindedly flicking through social media. I find myself on Noah's Facebook page. The post of the sunflower field remains the last thing he posted, and I cry all over again. How could I have been so stupid? I switch to messages. I compose and delete numerous messages because nothing seems quite right. I try the Noah approach, direct and honest.

C: Seems like these apology messages are becoming a regular occurrence. I don't want them to be. I cannot explain how sorry I am for what I said last night. There are no excuses. I just need you to know that I could NEVER regret meeting you. I understand if you never want to speak to me again xxx

Every minute that ticks by feels like a bit of my heart is being taken away with it. I have really messed things up this time. Half an hour passes, and Noah still doesn't message me back. I saw the "read receipt", so I know he saw it and is actively avoiding my texts. Knowing I'm getting the cold shoulder deliberately hurts the most. I deserve it though. I cry into my pillow. I want my mum; she would know how to make things better. She'd know just the right thing to say to make me feel as though my entire world isn't crashing down around me.

I stay in bed all day. Nanna tries coaxing me out with chocolate and ice cream, but I don't want to eat.

Dinner has come and gone by the time I make my way downstairs. It's eerily quiet. The twins have gone to bed, and Grandpa has fallen asleep on the couch next to Nanna. I creep into the kitchen and search the fridge for a cool drink. When I shut the door, I jump back with fright as Dad enters. We look at one another momentarily, neither one of us sure how to navigate this newfound awkwardness between us. He moves to the fridge and pulls out a tub of yoghurt before retreating from the kitchen without saying a word to me.

I'm surrounded by fractured relationships with people who mean the most to me, each shard cutting deeper with every new silent encounter. I don't want to live like this. I feel like I'm constantly shaking, not knowing what to expect from those around me or from myself. I think back to last night with Noah, and I don't recognise the girl I became over the summer: loving and caring one-minute, complete Irrational Psycho the next! I've never been anything but level-headed. In control. I feel so completely and utterly lost. I need to get out of the house. I've barely slept and now I'm over-tired, alone with my thoughts. They are unwelcome company.

I run upstairs to gather my things and call an Uber. I sneak out the back door, climb over the fence and run to a house a few doors down from my own. I gave the driver a different address so Nanna wouldn't see me sneak out. I haven't made up my mind where I'm going until I give the driver the new address, and even then, I'm still not sure it's the right thing to do.

The Uber pulls up outside the neat two-story house I know so well. It's late Monday night, and I'm suddenly aware of how inappropriate my visit might be. I seem to be making a habit of these lately, but time is moving differently. So much has happened in such a short space of time that it feels longer somehow, as though we should be further into the year but we're only mid-way through January. How can time move so slowly?

The lights are on in the main part of the house, so I'm filled with some form of hope that I'm not about to wake anyone. But it's not just the idea of waking up the household that's making me nervous; it's the fact that I might not be welcome here anymore. I hesitantly approach the door and knock. I hear muffled voices from the other side, questioning who would be calling so late. I nervously run my fingers through my hair and flash an apologetic smile as the door opens.

"Chelsea! I didn't expect to see you here this late. Is everything okay?"

I nod, thankful for the warm reception. "I know, I'm really sorry. I was hoping I could speak with Elliott. It's important."

"Of course, sweetheart, come in." Elliott's mother Claire has always been so kind to me. "He's up in his room. You can go up if you like."

I thank her and make my way up the familiar stairs. I find comfort in anything familiar right now. I spent many days here with Elliott before we were ever a thing, just hanging out. His house smells of cinnamon and looks like it came straight from the pages of a home magazine. Despite the show-home look, it feels homely. It is nice to know right now, that at least one thing hasn't changed.

I knock at his door and wait for the invitation to come in. As I enter, I find Elliott sprawled t on his bed, dressed down in tracksuit pants and a t-shirt watching TV. He sits up, surprised to see me.

"Chelsea! What are you doing here?" His eyes are wide, surprised. Is he also nervous?

"I need to talk to you."

His room hasn't changed at all. His large, queen bed sits to the left of the door, sheets messy and pillows thrown on the floor. Against the opposite wall is a dresser with a television on top. His desk sits below the window and is a mess with papers, clothes and odds and ends piled on top. His room is the complete opposite of the well put together guy we are all used to seeing. His floor though is clean which makes me think his mum was through earlier collecting his dirty washing. Right now, he looks like the Elliott I remember, the Elliott I liked best.

Elliott reaches for his phone and checks the time. "You needed to speak to me at 10.48 at night? You couldn't call?" he teases.

Elliott turns down the sound on his television and pats a spot beside him on the bed as an invitation to sit with him. I shake my head. I don't want to give him the wrong idea. I can see how this might look. "Before I sit there, I need to get something off my chest."

"Okay," he hesitates.

I lick my lips and let out a breath. "You were a real jerk to me after we broke up. This whole summer actually." I look to him for recognition, perhaps even for remorse. He looks sheepish, so I continue, "You really hurt me, Elliott. How you broke up with me, how you…you rubbed your hook ups in my face on social media, this thing with Willow and—"

"Yeah, I get it."

"Do you? Because I need you to really understand this. Elliott, you were my first boyfriend, and you really screwed me over, and before all of this you were one of my best friends. I just can't understand—"

He moves off the bed and takes my hand. "I know. I know and I feel really bad about it all. I do. And I'm sorry. I wish there was something bigger than sorry, but it's all I've got."

I know what he means. I wish I had something deeper, more meaningful to say to Noah, but there isn't anything. I clear my throat. I can't think about Noah right now. I need to get through this with Elliott first.

"I just need to know why. Why you dumped me? Why you were so mean afterwards? Why you pretended like what we had meant nothing to you? And why you used Willow? I need closure." I need to move on.

My inability to sleep and overworking brain made me realise that my issues with Noah stem from Elliott. As much as I try to ignore it, I'm still carrying Elliott-baggage and taking it into my relationship with Noah. Elliott smashed my trust, my confidence and my self-worth, and maybe, just maybe, if I get some answers off him then I can begin to heal and move on without my excess baggage. I don't want the remnants of my first relationship, and the broken relationship with my father, to carry over into all of my other relationships. Noah is too important to lose without a fight, and this is how I am going to fight for him; by finally fixing these old wounds and moving on for good.

Elliott drops one of my hands and reaches for the back of his neck, rubbing it as though he is uncomfortable. I plead with him to be honest, and he looks at me for a moment as if deciding if he should. He breaks the silence with a heavy sigh. "I don't know Chels. I don't have an answer for you."

It is not what I expect to hear. Or what I want. I wait. He looks to me for approval, to see if that is enough of an explanation. It's not. I'm not accepting that. He lets go of both my hands and flops backwards on his bed with a groan. "I thought I needed to be free after high school. Like having a girlfriend was weighing me down."

Ouch.

"It's not that I didn't have feelings for you anymore. I just wanted to let off some steam. I know that's a pretty shitty excuse, and I realised how much I still cared for you when you started hanging out with Kalani..."

I wait for more.

"And the rest of it…I don't know. Jealousy? Pride? Ego? Take your pick."

I want him to say he's going through something big, something personal so I can at least understand why he did the things he did, but there's nothing like that going on. He's coming across as a spoilt little boy who doesn't want his toy anymore but doesn't want anyone else to play with it either.

This is the best I'm going to get out of him, I realise, and I need to accept that. Perhaps people do things without good reasons, and those of us left wondering why, need to accept that and move on anyway. Maybe his reasons don't really matter. Maybe it's just how I deal with it that matters. It occurs to me that this is what Noah was trying to teach me all along.

I am in control.

I can have these fractured relationships and be okay, get on with my life. I am only one half of these relationships. I can't control what Elliott did or said any more than I can my own father, but I can control what *I* do and what *I* say. I can only control me.

As much as I want Elliott to give me an answer so I can heal, he can't give it to me, and I can't give him the power to leave me broken. I have to heal anyway. I am not what happens to me. I can define myself, my future and my relationships however *I* want. Noah is not Elliott, and he is not my father. He has proved this time and time again, yet I keep testing him like he is. I have to let go of all of this and treat Noah as Noah. If I fall and get hurt again, then I'll dust myself off and get back up. Noah lives his life by trusting people, being honest and not letting his past colour his future. Now, I'm determined to do the same.

"I forgive you," I say to Elliott, surprising us both. "What you did and the things you said were not okay, don't get me wrong. But I'm forgiving you for my own peace."

He looks confused and unsure what to say next. I don't hang around. I have nothing more I want to say.

I have somewhere else I need to be.

THIRTY-ONE

In the back of my second Uber ride for the night, I smile to myself, satisfied that I have finally closed the "Elliott Chapter" of my life. He's no longer allowed to occupy any space in my mind or my heart. Tonight, he's shown just what a selfish and entitled child he is. I don't want to be like that. I want to stop this back and forth fighting with Noah. I know it's all my doing. It's because I've been all over the place with my emotions and trying to process everything that has happened since I finished school. I also know that Noah has been nothing but supportive and deserves better. I want to be better. I will be better. By closing that phase of my life, I already feel taller. I just hope that Noah can find it in his generous heart to forgive me one last time so I can show him how ready I am to be the better me.

I have no idea how Noah is going to react to seeing me or if he *will* even see me, but I have to try. I definitely do not want to knock on the front door and wake his grandparents up, and I don't want to try my luck with Banner around the side, so I send Noah a message telling him I'm outside his house. My phone vibrates in my hand, reminding me that I have the sound off. I'm surprised to see it is actually ringing. I answer the call.

"I'm not home." His voice is gruff and a little annoyed.

"Well, I'm here, and I'll wait for you."

A pause. Followed by a sigh. His. "I might be a while."

"Then I'll wait a while."

"You've got me on the line, why not just tell me now?" his voice is softening, but it's still tainted by frustration.

"I didn't come out here at midnight to talk to you on the phone. This is important. Face to face."

"Thought you didn't like confrontation."

"Does it have to be confrontational?" I hope he can hear the plea in my voice.

"Everything seems to be lately."

Ouch. I don't respond. I deserved that. I wait for him to speak. He sighs, and I can hear him rubbing his beard in thought on the other end.

"Gimme fifteen."

I smile. "I'll be here."

"I know, Roberts, I know."

He hangs up, and I do a small victory dance. "Roberts." It makes me smile.

An unfamiliar car pulls up to the curb a short while later. A woman is behind the wheel, and I feel a stabbing pain in my chest. I resist the urge to ask who she is and where exactly he has been. He folds out of the sedan, hair back, dressed in black jeans and a hoodie. He leans into the window and says something to the driver that makes her smile before driving off. I can't stop the pang of jealousy in the pit of my stomach. He looks after the car before turning to me, hands in his pockets, slowly closing the gap between us. Every inch of my body is aching to be held by him. He stops, right in my personal space, looking down at me with kind eyes that I don't deserve. I drink in his scent (sage and beer). I run my eyes over him. He gives me a crooked smile.

"She's my mate's wife. He was too drunk to give me a lift."

"You don't owe me an explanation."

He chuckles. "I know you were dying to know." I give him a small smile. Check mate. "Alright Roberts, what is so important that you pulled me away from drowning my sorrows?" Sass, maybe there was hope yet.

I clear my throat. *This is it, Chelsea, clear and simple. You got this.* "I…I…urgh, I don't know where to start!" I throw my hands in the air.

He looks at me expectantly, slightly mocking me, waiting for me to pull myself together.

"I'm just going to come out with it."

"Go right ahead," he says.

"I'm sorry. I'm really, really sorry. If there was a bigger word than sorry, I would use it because sorry doesn't seem to cover it. I was so mean to you, and I'm sorry. I kept expecting you to be like Elliott, or my dad, and you're not. You're nothing like them. You're amazing. And I love you so much. I don't regret stopping to talk—"

Noah presses his lips to mine, slowly parting them. His tongue moves in perfect rhythm with mine; his hands come up to cup my face. He pulls me in closer, and I throw my arms around his neck, pressing my lips harder against his. We part and he rests his forehead against mine.

"I'm sorry," I whisper.

"You said that," he grins at me. "Chels, I can't keep doing this. The fighting and getting back together—"

"I know, I know. It's going to stop. I realise now what has been going on, and I'm fixing it. I just want to be with you. I love you, and I don't want to keep fighting or pushing you away."

"Say it again," he whispers.

"I'm sorry."

He shakes his head. "The love part."

"I love you."

He kisses me, and I melt into him.

I stay the night with Noah, and it isn't until Nanna calls me the next morning that I remember that she and Grandpa would have been expecting me to be asleep in my own bed. I answer the call, apologising profusely. Once Nanna calms down, she orders me back home immediately. Mum is coming home today.

"You heard right. She rang this morning and said she'll be home just after lunch. So, get a wriggle on and get home before she does!"

I nod before remembering that she can't see me. "Okay, I'll be right there."

I hang up the phone and turn to Noah. "Mum's coming home. I have to go."

THIRTY-TWO

Arriving home from anywhere usually results in a warm, fuzzy feeling, like the weight of the world has been lifted off my shoulders. It's a refuge from the outside world. Lately though, arriving home means nausea and a tightening in my chest. It is the war zone. Today is no different. I feel so sick as Noah pulls into our driveway, I think I might actually vomit in his car. I have no idea what to expect from Mum. She has ignored all of my attempts at contacting her since she's been away. I know she is mad at me. I feel responsible for her heartbreak. I want, so desperately, to walk through the front door and have everything back the way it was, but I know it is not.

It's a funny feeling knowing that your life is never going to be the same again. For the last seventeen years my life has been predictable, even my future pre-planned. Every night I'd come home from school and see a glimpse of my future in Mum and Dad. Now, all that is gone. I don't know what the future looks like anymore. I don't know where I fit, where any of us fit. I have no idea what is waiting for me on the other side of those doors to the place I once called home, but at least I'm not alone.

I have Noah.

He's my home now.

Last night we talked about everything. I was brutally honest with him and myself, for exactly how I've handled everything. He was much easier on me than I was. We made a promise to each other to always be open and honest, no matter what. I made the extra promise to stop pushing him away every time I freak out.

I lace my fingers through his and we walk in together. Everyone is gathered in the front lounge room waiting for Mum. They are disappointed when they see it's just us walking through the door. I'm not offended. I'm anxiously awaiting her arrival too.

My brothers and father, who is now showered and cleanly shaved, are noticeably on edge. Dad is fidgeting with a paper weight, turning it over in his hands. The twins are practically sitting on top of each other, shouldering one another out of the way for more space on the couch. It's clear they haven't heard from Mum either during her absence. Grandpa sits stoned-faced, reading the newspaper in the corner, and Nanna tries to keep us together by offering food and drink. No one has the stomach for it, so it sits on the coffee table, untouched. We sit in silence and find our own spot on the carpet to stare at. I grip Noah's hand tighter, and he pats my leg with his free hand. I don't think I could get through this without him here.

The sound of heels clicking on the concrete outside grab everyone's attention. Our eyes dart to the front door. The doorknob turns, and Mum walks in, looking like she's stepped off the cover of *Vogue* or something. It's not what I am expecting at all. Judging by everyone's faces, it's not what any of us are expecting. Her hair is glossy and blow waved, she is wearing bright red lipstick, a tight pencil skirt and a flowy white blouse that is slightly see through. I turn to Noah. He subtly shrugs his shoulders. This doesn't look good. I mean, she looked great, but the situation is not looking good.

"Hi," she smiles at us all although avoiding direct contact with anyone, "Noah, nice to see you." He nods in response.

I look over at Dad who is as openly shocked as I feel. His mouth is agape, his brows furrowed. During Mum's absence, Dad spent most of his time in his room. The rare times he wasn't in his room, he moped around the house, never showering or shaving, and wearing clothes with holes in them. He didn't eat with us or even speak to us. He looked as if he'd aged fifteen years, and although he is better presented today, he still looks terrible. Just old and tired, while Mum looks like a million bucks. A new wave of nausea sweeps over me as I realise what this means. They are breaking up, and she is going to win the divorce; show him what he's lost.

"What are you all doing, sitting around acting like someone died?" She walks over and sits with the twins, pulling them in for a hug, telling them how much she missed them. Still, no one says anything. Grandpa puts down the newspaper and stares like the rest of us.

"Does anyone want to fill me in on what I've missed? What have you been up to?" Her eyes bore into Noah and me, and I see she is barely holding it together. She is trying to appear calm and collected in front of us all but underneath all that hair and make-up is a woman about to break. She is looking to us to help prop her up.

"Nothing much," I manage to say back to her.

An awkward silence fills the room. No-one knows what to say next. We give each other hurried looks, silently begging each other to speak and break this suffocating silence. The avoidance of the elephant in the room is making me dizzy. I don't want to be the one to speak. I've caused enough damage by doing that, but the silence is getting to me.

"So, what's going on? What does this mean?" The words come out before I register that they escaped from my mouth. Noah squeezes my hand in support.

Mum looks at me blankly, and Dad keeps his eyes on her, trying to figure it out before the rest of us.

"I think," Nanna injects, "what Chelsea is trying to say is, how are you, Helena? We've all been worried about you since none of us have heard from you. You look," Nanna searches for the right word and settles on, "great."

"I'm doing the best I can under the circumstances," Mum's tone changes and her words have more edge to them. "I needed some time on my own to think before I was ready to come home to my children."

"Children? Just the children?" Dad asks although he shouldn't have.

"Yes Andrew, just the children. I expect you have somewhere else you can go." She turns on him like an ice queen. My heart flips.

"Go? You want me to leave?"

"I think it's for the best right now, don't you? School will start soon, and the boys could use a calm environment for the beginning of the school year. Plus, I'll need to help Chelsea get ready for her trip to Europe."

I do a double take. *What?*

"I didn't know she was going," Dad says through gritted teeth.

"Well, she is," Mum adds defiantly. She dares him to speak again.

"I am?"

"Yes, honey, your father will pay for it. It's a fantastic opportunity for you both. Go and experience the world and decide what you want out of life. You shouldn't be forced to stay here and do something you don't want to do." A double strike.

Dad recoils at her words, understanding the double meaning. Noah stays silent. Wise choice. My head is spinning.

"So, that's it. You've decided all this?" Dad raises his voice.

"Yes. For once, Andrew, I've made a decision about what is best for our family." There are years of suppressed anger and sadness in her voice. "We have a lot to still talk about and work through, and I don't think that can be done while you're living here. There's no need for Chelsea to be here if she doesn't have to be. The boys deserve to jump back into routine without disruption. I don't think this is too much to ask, do you?" It is a challenge that Dad is smart enough not to take on.

We sit in stunned silence, looking at the woman sitting before us. She is determined and strong, and I like it. I've never admired my mum more than I do right at this moment. She's a powerful force to be reckoned with. Dad leaves the lounge room to pack his belongings while Mum gets up and potters around the house, all the while assuring Nanna that she is fine. The twins make themselves scarce, and I feel like I've sustained whiplash from the speed at which things go back to normal. There's no yelling, no fighting, no demand making; just a clear-cut decision.

Dad's moving out.

Mum's now in control.

I wonder how much yelling and fighting happened in Sydney for it to be like this now. I struggle with what all this means, with the calmness. I don't know what to do with myself, so I take Noah to my room, hoping he has more insight into what is going on.

"Your mum is a total badass," he says as he sits on my bed.

"Yeah, I didn't know she had it in her." I curl up next to him, chewing my lip, thinking over everything that just happened.

"She was awesome. Put your dad in his place."

"Hmmm…," is all I can manage. It's a lot to process. Noah puts his arms around me and kisses the top of my head. "And you're coming to Europe with me!"

"Yeah…" I say, still a million miles away.

If Mum has kicked Dad out of the house, does this mean they are definitely getting a divorce? She said they had some things to talk through, but did she mean like divorce things or saving our marriage things? The status of our family is still unclear. I need answers. I need to know what this means. If I'm really going overseas with Noah (am I?) then I need to know what the next steps are back here. I need to know what it is I'm leaving behind. I tell Noah to wait in my room and wander downstairs to find my mum, sitting back in the kitchen flipping through a magazine with a large glass of red wine in front of her. It's a little early in the afternoon to be drinking, but who am I to judge a woman whose husband has a secret family.

"Mum?" my voice is unsteady.

She turns around to face me. "Oh, hey, Chels," she says, as if surprised to see me there. She motions for me to come over and sit next to her. I do.

Mum takes a large sip of her drink. I'm concerned. She doesn't look like Mum and she's not acting like Mum. I can't remember the last time I saw her drink, let alone drink in the middle of the day. Is it really a good idea for me to be going overseas right now? Doesn't she need me?

"Are you and Dad getting a divorce?" I surprise myself with the directness of my question. Noah must be rubbing off on me.

She throws her hands up and lets out a small laugh. "Yes. No. Who knows?" Is she drunk already? "Chelsea, your father and I have a lot to talk about and figure out. I don't know what will happen." She takes another big swig.

"I'm sorry."

She throws her arms around me and pulls me in close. "Oh, honey, none of this is your fault. None."

My cheeks feel wet. "I just—"

"Shhh…," she soothes me. I feel guilty. Shouldn't I be comforting her?

"I don't have to go to Europe, Mum. I can stay here—"

"You'll do no such thing, Miss Chelsea May."

"But don't you need me?" It comes out as a plea instead of as a question.

She smiles. "Oh, honey, this is not your mess to fix. I'm," she waves her hands over herself, "not your mess to fix. That's what I have girlfriends for." She winks at me.

I can see a slight shake to her hands as she holds her wine glass. She is barely holding it together. I can't leave her like this.

"Sweetheart, go to Europe. Have an adventure with your boyfriend. Be young and free. Don't worry about all this; it'll still be here when you get back."

Will it though? "What about Dad?"

She waves away the thought. "He'll always be your father. Regardless of what happens between us, you get to decide what sort of relationship you want with him. Maybe some time away will give you the perspective you need to make the decision."

"Aren't you mad?" It's not my place, but I ask anyway because she doesn't seem mad. If it were me, I'd be mad as hell!

"I am," she swallows, fighting back tears, "I'm heartbroken."

I shake my head, still trying to understand what happened. How could this happen to our family? I ask her, and she pauses, as if selecting her words carefully.

"Honey, your father and I haven't been *us* in a really long time. I guess he got so caught up in his work and his promotion, and I was needed here." So this was our fault, mine and the twins. Guilt swirls in my stomach. "Your father and I drifted apart. It happens."

"But that doesn't mean he had to start a family with someone else!"

"No, it doesn't, and our problems don't excuse his actions, but I need to have a look at my part in this too. We became more like co-parents rather than husband and wife."

"So what, he just found someone else?" I shake my head in disbelief.

Mum shrugs. "He never meant for it to turn into anything serious."

"But it did. A whole other family with two kids!" I say with my anger on show.

Mum takes a swig of her drink and swallows. "One kid. The little girl isn't his. She's the product of a whole other messy, on again, off again relationship." She shakes her head dismissively.

"So, now what?"

"I don't have the answers you want right now, Chelsea. I don't know…I don't know." Our tears fall in unison. "Listen to me, Chelsea; there's nothing you can do here. We all need time. Hell, maybe I'll bring the boys, and we'll join you over there!" She smiles at me. "Go honey."

I give her a hug like the ones I used to give her when I was younger, the ones I thought I had outgrown. It's comforting.

I have no idea how I feel about my father right now and what sort of relationship I want with him. I don't know if I can forgive him. I don't know if I want to meet Miss Glossy Hair and their son. Part of me wants to forget that they even exist, and yet another part of me would like to get to know his other kid. I hate that part of me. I feel like I'm betraying Mum by even thinking about it. I don't recall his face in detail from the trip to the zoo, but I can't help wondering if we look similar or have any of the same traits. I also feel guilty for wanting to know that. Right now, today, I don't have the answers. I don't know what I want. I don't know whether my family will stay intact, or if I will ever have a relationship with my father again. And I'm trying to be okay with not knowing. I'm learning that I don't need to have all the answers right now.

THIRTY-THREE

The airport is a hive of activity. People are buzzing everywhere; running to catch flights, reuniting with loved ones, or saying their last frantic goodbyes to those departing. Our farewell party is small. Noah said goodbye to his grandparents at home, so they didn't have to fight the city traffic and scores of people at the airport. His nan is still recovering from hip surgery, after all. Noah found it hardest of all to say goodbye to Banner. That dog has only just begun to trust me, and here I am, running away with his person. But Noah is my person too. I guess we'll just have to share him. At least Noah is comforted by the fact that Banner will be there to watch over his grandparents in his absence.

Mum drives us in and holds it together right up until we are ready to walk through to the International Departure lounge.

She repeatedly asks if we have everything and proceeds to list them again. She's triple-checked we have our passports and boarding passes. It would have been annoying if it wasn't the last time that I'm going to see her in goodness knows how long.

She and Dad have agreed to go to counselling. Mum isn't sure if she wants to save her marriage, but she told me that she owes it to herself to see where it takes them. Dad hasn't been at the house since that day. I haven't really spoken to him, but he did send me a message this morning wishing both of us a safe trip. I guess that's something. I learned that Miss Glossy Hair's name is Amanda, and that my half-brother's name is Daniel. I haven't met them yet.

My actual brothers, though, currently have their heads buried deep in their Switches, daring to quickly look up and say goodbye before the zombies attack their troops or whatever. They do manage to make demands though, about being brought back gifts when I eventually return.

"Are you sure you've got everything? Tickets? Passports?" Mum goes through her routine again as we approach the gates.

"Yes! Relax Mum!"

"Don't worry, Helena, I'll take good care of her."

"Be sure you do, Noah, or I'll jump on the next plane over and sort you out myself," she teases. Mum's eyes start to give way to the tears she has been holding back.

"You think she's joking," I say flatly to Noah, "she's not."

"We'll be fine." he reassures us.

Mum pulls us both in for one last hug, one last reminder to be safe, and one last passport check. I give her a kiss and tell her I love her. It sets off a new round of tears, and now I'm struggling to hold it together myself. Noah laces his fingers through mine and gently pulls me away knowing that if he doesn't do so, we won't leave. I wave one last time as we walk through the first checkpoint.

"Ready, Roberts?" he winks at me.

I run my hands through my freshly cut, baby-pink hair. "Absolutely."

Acknowledgements

Writing and publishing my own book has been a lifelong dream, so my very first thank you must indeed go to you, dear reader, for reading my book! I am very grateful for you.

Mum – thank you for introducing me to books and for always saying 'yes' whenever I asked to buy one as a child. You have been one of my biggest supporters from the very first time I was brave enough to share my dream of becoming an author and I cannot thank you enough for your love and support. I hope I've made you proud.

Rob – how did I get so lucky? Thank you for keeping me hydrated with copious amounts of hot chocolates as I tapped away at my laptop and for encouraging me to follow my dreams. Your support means everything to me.

Maya, Alex and Samara – thank you for sharing me with my fictional worlds. I hope I make you proud and show you that it's never too late to follow your dreams. I love you beyond words.

Dad and Barb – hey look! I wrote a book! Thank you for your love and support.

Laura – you've been in my corner, cheering me on since the very first draft (and even before then, from when I first started dreaming of this day) and I thank you from the bottom of my heart for all of your words (texts, memes and gifs) of encouragement, advice, guidance and expert use of semicolons. As a show of my appreciation, I shall shower you with Chris Pine/Evans memes for all eternity.

To my editor, Laura Boon – you were so wonderful to work with. Thank you for your kind words and helping me make this the best version of Chelsea's story. (Disclaimer – I cheekily did not show Laura my 'Acknowledgements' page so all errors are my own) I look forward to working with you again soon.

To Emily Folkard – I'm still trying to figure out how you managed to turn my terrible drawing and rambling emails into the most incredible pieces of art that sit on the front and back covers of my book! Thank you so much for being patient and learning about cover sizing along with me. The art you have created for the book is nothing short of stunning. Here's to the next project!

Thank you to the rest of my friends and family who have supported me, encouraged me and generally made me feel like a total super star. Never underestimate the power of kindness and lifting one another up. Big love.

A huge thank you to Danielle Binks, Justine Barker, Nicola Santilli and Luna Soo who gave me wonderful feedback and encouragement on this story and writing in general. Thank you to Ellie Marney for one of the best writing and publishing workshops I have ever done; your workshop gave me the confidence and the know-how to follow my dreams. Thank you.

To all the bookstagramers, bloggers, vloggers, librarians, book sellers, teachers and book lovers that continue to talk about books and put books in the hands of others, thank you. What a dull world it would be without the gift of story.

About the Author

Katie Montinaro is a Melbourne-based writer and teacher. After many years of teaching her students how to write and craft narratives, Katie finally took the plunge and followed her lifelong dream of writing and publishing her books. When she's not writing she can be found reading, enjoying the cinemas or designing something new for her husband to build around the house. Katie loves nothing more than hanging out with her kids and dog, Arthur - unless Jason Momoa were to call…she'd definitely prefer to go on a date with Aquaman. Sorry, kids!

Katie would love to connect with her readers, so make sure you drop by and say hi! Keep up to date with Katie's writing on her website and social media accounts.

www.katiemontinaro.com

www.ingramcontent.com/pod-product-compliance
Lightning Source LLC
Chambersburg PA
CBHW020133120726
47903CB00007B/2240